"You're not easy to assess," he said

"We must get to know each other better."

"Must we?" Livvy echoed. Her eyes met his searching intensity, and she wondered wildly what he could see.

"We could start with dinner tonight. And talk."

She thought fleetingly of Andrew, who was not going to like this, and then shock took over as Colin kissed her.

He knew how to kiss. It took a real effort not to respond and let the delicious sensations go on and on.

It could be fascinating getting to know him, but she must always remember what she was hiding and never let him get close to that. Nor too close to her, now that a kiss had shown her what effect he could have on her.

Jane Donnelly, a former journalist, lives in a picture-perfect cottage just outside Stratford-upon-Avon with her daughter and their assortment of pets. She has written everything from short stories to movie scripts and has developed into a prolific author of warmhearted romance novels since she started to write for Harlequin in 1968. She finds her writer's life immensely satisfying, loves the excuse to travel and still has a reporter's instinct for gathering news and scribbling down notes, which she later uses in her books.

Books by Jane Donnelly

HARLEQUIN ROMANCE

Don't miss any of our special offers. Write to us at the following address for information on our newest releases.

Harlequin Reader Service
901 Fuhrmann Blvd., P.O. Box 1397, Buffalo, NY 14240
Canadian address: P.O. Box 603,
Fort Erie, Ont. L2A 5X3

When We're Alone

Jane Donnelly

Harlequin Books

TORONTO • NEW YORK • LONDON
AMSTERDAM • PARIS • SYDNEY • HAMBURG
STOCKHOLM • ATHENS • TOKYO • MILAN

Original hardcover edition published in 1989
by Mills & Boon Limited

ISBN 0-373-03033-9

Harlequin Romance first edition February 1990

CHAPTER ONE

'So who did it?' the girl demanded. The child went on howling. The two Siamese cats stared unblinkingly, then the smaller sauntered away, disdain in every line.

The larger sidled up to Livvy, looking guilty, and she sighed. 'Oh, Mischa, that was very bad!'

Daisy, aged four, had been scratched. There was a tiny pink line on her little plump leg, and immediately following her first screech on the landing outside she had been bundled in here by her mother, who had announced, 'One of them's *scratched* her!' as though it was a mortal wound.

Sonia Baines was the over-protective mum of a mischievous tot. Daisy had either teased or hugged the cat too tightly, but Sonia always reacted as if never, in any way, could her darling be at fault. Now she clasped Daisy to her, crooning, 'Poor baby, then,' and Livvy suggested wearily,

'Dab some TCP on it.'

She opened the bathroom cabinet and took out a bottle, and Daisy's screams rose higher while Sonia dithered. 'It won't hurt, Mummy won't let it hurt.' Then Daisy struck out, sending the bottle flying to smash on the tiled floor and splash up the wall.

Livvy was decorating the room. It was one of her winter chores in this guesthouse, and she could have done without disinfectant on the still tacky pale blue wall. 'Oh, darling!' Sonia wailed.

'Oh, *hell*!' Livvy muttered, and Daisy shut up, bright enough to realise that had not been a clever move.

A man loomed in the doorway. White-bearded and ruddy-faced, he looked what he was, a retired sailor. 'No use calling,' he said. 'Take a foghorn to make itself heard with the racket that's going on in here. What's the damage this time?'

Daisy raised her leg and he stooped and stared, grizzled brows meeting. 'Where?'

'Mischa scratched her!' Sonia cried, and he wagged a finger at Daisy.

'Ah, but what did she do to Mischa, eh? And there's a feller outside asking for Miss Murrin.'

That was Livvy, who hesitated for a moment, wondering whether to dab the wet paint where the liquid was running, or let it dry and then assess the damage. 'What's he want?' she asked.

'No idea, m'dear. Just returning from my constitutional when this station wagon drew up and this feller got out.'

Daisy began to wail again and the Captain said, 'That's enough of that,' and Sonia crooned, 'Let Mummy kiss it better.'

Mischa went too, close as a shadow to Livvy's bare feet as she padded out on to the landing and down the staircase into the big, bright entrance hall. The girl moved as gracefully as a cat herself. She was tallish and slim, with fair, straight hair falling over her shoulders, high cheekbones and blue, slightly slanted eyes.

The hall was empty, the front door open, and there was a station wagon drawn up on the forecourt. Mischa, still needing reassurance that all was forgiven, brushed Livvy's ankles and, when she paused at the top of the steps leading down from the front door, threaded between her legs so that she lurched down.

She landed awkwardly but on her feet, and straightened at once. It was the cat that went sprawling, and a man said, 'I thought cats always fell on their feet.'

'Siamese sometimes have a poor sense of balance,' she said. 'What can we do for you?'

He had been standing by the old red brick wall that overlooked the gardens, and now he strode across, and something about him took her breath away. He was unusually tall, broad-shouldered, his hair dark and unruly, his face dark and lean. He was looking hard at her, and when he smiled, his teeth white against the tan of his skin, her answering smile was twitchy. She said, 'If you're looking for accommodation, I'm sorry, but we're closed.'

At the back of the car a dog began to bark furiously as Mischa swaggered up and down. Livvy knew there was no danger of the dog getting out, because if there had been you wouldn't have seen Mischa for dust.

'That's a brave cat,' said the man.

Mischa was acting very butch, daring the dog to do its worst, and Livvy said, 'That is a cat of no courage at all. You go to open the door and see him move. Do I know you?'

She felt she should, and she had a good memory for faces. She would surely have remembered him, but his 'No' sounded definite enough. So he was probably looking for somewhere to stay, and Sweet Orchard Farm—which had not been a farm for over twenty years—shut for the season at the end of September. It was late November now, and she began, 'If you're on holiday, I can recommend——'

'I'm here to see Miss Murrin.'

He didn't wait for her to finish, interrupting in the way of someone who has no qualms about talking down anybody, and her, 'You're seeing her,' took on a brisker note.

'Miss Maybelle Murrin.'

'Ah!' Aunt Maysie was not expecting any callers this morning, although there was no good reason why Livvy should not take him up to the apartment where Maybelle was reading the Sunday newspapers. But a sudden chill was running down her spine.

Her cat-sense, Aunt Maysie called it. Sometimes it seemed that Livvy got hunches like that—a warning system when danger was near.

From the booming sound of barking that was a big dog. It was the man, not the dog, who was sounding alarm bells in her mind, but she called, 'Mischa, come away from there!' and walked to the back of the wagon to scoop up the Siamese. '*Is* that a dog?' she gasped.

The big shaggy head could have passed for a yeti. The man said, 'Name of Luke.'

'Hi, Luke. Come away, Mischa, you fool! Suppose you met him on a dark night?' She carried the cat back to the house and tipped him on to the steps, and the man looked down at her bare feet and silvered toenails and asked, 'Can you walk over red-hot coals as well?'

The shingle of the forecourt contained some sharp stones, but Livvy had walked the rocky coastline barefoot from a child. As a hotelier she dressed smartly, and certainly in shoes, but she was happy shoeless. She turned mocking blue eyes on him. 'You know, I never thought of that. Maybe I could. We have barbecues here, I could do a cabaret turn.'

He laughed. 'You will practise before you jump in feet first? I wouldn't like to be the cause of you going up in smoke.'

'No danger,' she said gaily. 'I'm flame-proof. Come in.'

From the red-flagstoned floor to the polished brass on the gleaming table, the old oil paintings and the chintz-covered settle, it still looked like the hallway of a comfortably off farming family. 'In here,' said Livvy, and opened a door.

The office had not changed much either. There was a filing cabinet, a typewriter and a small word processor, but the wallpaper of tiny trailing roses was a reproduction, and the furniture had been in the house before Aunt Maysie had been born here.

Livvy seated herself behind a rosewood desk and said, 'Do sit down.'

He took the chair facing her across the desk, sitting right back, elbows on the chair arms, fingers loosely linked. His hands looked strong. She looked at them first before she raised her eyes to meet his eyes, which were hooded and watchful. He was a striking man. It was a hard face, the skin taut over high Red Indian cheekbones and a mouth without curve until he smiled. Then the charm worked. 'My name's Corbin Radbrook,' he introduced himself, and that clicked into place in her mind.

Radbrook? Corbin Radbrook, of *course*! She said, 'You're the writer,' as he said, 'I'm doing some research for a TV series.'

TV was where she might have seen him. Or in a magazine or a newspaper. He did investigative journalism into crimes and scandals, turning out books, articles, scripts. And he looked the part—tough and uncompromising.

'Down here,' he went on, 'I'm following up a story that happened sixty years ago when a young artist died. A Laurence Charles.' She nodded. 'You know about it?'

'Not a lot. It was a long time ago. TV, did you say? Tell me more.' She wasn't sure he was fooled by the flattery, but she listened, lips parted and eyes widening.

'There are going to be four hour-long scripts. Murders and likely murders where a woman was at the heart of things—Lizzie Borden, Florence Bravo, Madeleine Smith. Three well-known lethal ladies, and ending with a story that's been forgotten. I'm adding the Dark Lady to the list.'

'The who?'

'That was what the press was asking at the time, who is the Dark Lady? There was a painting of a girl with raven hair that was all but destroyed.'

Livvy nodded again. 'I think I've heard of that, but why do you want to talk to Aunt Maysie? She wasn't an artist, she was a farmer's daughter. I don't think she knew any of them.' There had once been a community of artists and sculptors living near here, but they had dispersed years and years ago.

'They were both on a photograph that was taken at a garden party,' he told her. 'One of the local papers at the time published it. That was how I got her name, going through the files.'

And she bubbled with false enthusiasm, 'Was there a *photograph*? Oh, I'd like to see that. My name's Olivia Murrin, by the way, everyone calls me Livvy. My great-grandfather and Maybelle were brother and sister.'

'I'm delighted to meet you.' He held out a hand, his fingers taking hers in a cool firm clasp, and she felt as if the palm of her hand was sweating.

'My pleasure,' she said gaily, and went on confidingly, 'But I don't think you'll get much from Aunt Maysie. She's very frail and her mind tends to wander.' What lies she was telling! 'She's very old—well, she would be, wouldn't she? And she has a heart condition, so any sort of stress triggers trouble, and I would like to see her doctor about her giving interviews.'

He could hardly object to that, and he said, 'Of course.'

'Thank you.' Livvy flashed her most seductive smile that rarely failed. 'Will there be filming down here?' She sounded thrilled.

'Very probably.' An eyebrow raised. 'You're not a resting actress, by any chance?'

'Not by any chance.' Although she was putting on a good act now. 'Running this place takes all my time and energy. Have you done the other scripts?'

'Lizzie and Florence are in the bag, and I'm almost through with Madeleine.'

'Oh, I've heard of her.' She practically clapped her hands, giving herself a round of applause. 'The girl with the cocoa.'

'That she was.'

'Puts you off cocoa, doesn't it?'

'I was never on it.'

She tilted her head so that her silver ash hair fell forward in a smooth curtain. Her eyes danced. 'You don't look like a cocoa man, and you do look too cynical to have taken anything Madeleine was offering that night.'

Madeleine Smith was one of the belles of Glasgow in the 1850s, until she tired of her secret lover and he became a threat to her plans. The evidence was that he had gone to Madeleine's home in the darkness, and she had passed him a cup of cocoa through the bars of her basement bedroom not long before he died of arsenic poisoning. But the verdict was 'Not Proven', and Madeleine had walked free.

'She must have been quite a girl,' said Corbin Radbrook. 'But you're right, I wouldn't have touched her cocoa with a bargepole.'

'It makes a good story,' Livvy said gaily. 'Our Dark Lady will be in lively company.'

They were getting on well, as if he had liked her on sight. 'So please will you leave it till tomorrow?' she entreated. 'I'll have a word with Dr Aslett, and if you come along in the afternoon, say about three, we could talk about it.'

She was making a date with him, using the full force of her fascination.

'About three,' he said.

'Where are you staying?' Now she sounded regretful. 'I'm sorry we're closed. I wish you could have stayed here, but everything's under dust sheets. And I'm in the middle of redecorating, as you can see.' She stood up, displaying the paint splashes on her jeans and shirt, and he stood too, apologising for disturbing her.

'Think nothing of it,' she said, although it had been one body blow after another. 'Where *are* you staying?'

'At the Crow's Nest.' That was a motel a few miles away.

'You should be cosy there. Till tomorrow, then—and enjoy yourself with Madeleine.' Mischief lit her face. 'Do you suppose Emile's friends said that, before it all ended in cocoa and tears?'

He chuckled, and they went together out of the office and the house, and Livvy stood on the steps, waving as the station wagon drew away, with the great shaggy head of the dog turned towards her.

Then her hand dropped heavily to her side and the smile stiffened on her lips. When she walked back into the hall, Daisy and Sonia were coming downstairs. Daisy's leg sported a Band-Aid, and Sonia said, 'It was Schula.'

'What was?'

'Schula scratched Daisy.'

Mischa was the one with the guilt complex. When the screaming started, Mischa would panic. 'That doesn't surprise me,' said Livvy, fed up with all this fuss over nothing. 'I'll be ringing Dr Aslett later, do you want me to arrange a rabies jab?'

Horror transfixed Sonia, and Daisy, who had been enjoying herself up to now, looked up at her mother open-mouthed. 'That isn't funny,' Sonia said stiffly.

'So shut up about it,' said Livvy. 'She'll live.'

Livvy was not usually like this, but now she passed them on the stairs stony-faced, and Sonia asked, 'Anything the matter?'

'Could be,' said Livvy.

When Sonia's husband had walked out on her, leaving her in London in a flat on which rent was owing, no money and a two-year-old child, Livvy had been her salvation. They were old polytechnic friends who had kept in touch, and Livvy's offer of somewhere to stay while Sonia got herself together had seemed a godsend. So much so that once she was here she couldn't face the thought of leaving. Now she helped with the cooking during the holiday season and she and Daisy were permanent residents all year round, part of the family.

The guesthouse paid its way and Livvy was generous. Not much troubled her, she took most things in her stride. When Livvy said something was wrong and looked so grim about it, Sonia got butterflies in her stomach. She went after her, enquiring quite timorously, 'Is it money?'

Livvy stopped and turned to face her friend. Sonia was a plain girl who could have been prettier, with a round, pale face devoid of make-up, mousy brown hair parted in the middle and drawn into a loose coil at the back of her neck. Now her eyes and the twist of her lips were fearful, and Livvy made herself smile reassuringly, 'No, nothing like that.' She left Sonia standing and went through a door that stood ajar into one of the bedrooms.

Captain Henry Webb, late of the Merchant Navy, had been a paying guest here for as long as Livvy could remember, and the room was a larger edition of a ship's cabin; even the bed looked like a bunk.

The panelled walls were hung with pictures of ships and charts, except for those that supported ceiling-to-floor bookshelves. A mounted telescope stood in the square tower of a window alcove, and Livvy looked around. 'Henry?'

The room was empty, and she went to the telescope, swinging it to focus on the road that led along the clifftop to the small town. The station wagon had been drawn up on the verge not far from the house. The dog was galloping to and fro, looking not unlike a shaggy pony. The man was leaning against the car, arms folded, looking back. The powerful lens brought him so close that he could have been only an arm's distance away, and suddenly his eyes seemed to meet hers and she gasped. He must be looking towards this window, although there was no sun to flash on the telescope.

He couldn't see her, but he was very still, as if he was watching. What was he thinking? What was he waiting for? Livvy stepped back hastily and her hands were shaking so that she stood in the middle of the room for a minute or two before she came out again.

In her office she dialled the doctor's number, and she was lucky there. He answered himself, and she was talking to an old friend; when she said, 'It's about Aunt Maybelle,' she knew that she would have all his attention and his concern.

She said, 'A man's just turned up who wants to talk to her.' She told him why, and he asked, 'What's the problem?'

'The problem's the writer. His name's Corbin Radbrook.'

'I've heard of him. He's good.'

'He's trouble. And I feel that a sickroom is the last place he should be let loose in.'

She knew that Clifford Aslett was smiling. 'Maybelle wouldn't appreciate hearing her apartment described as a sickroom, nor if we started vetting her visitors. If she doesn't want to see him that must be her choice, but I can see no harm in it.'

She almost shrieked at him, but she had to stay calm. 'Suppose they want to bring in TV cameras and crews?'

'We'll cross that bridge when we come to it.'

'But you won't advise against her seeing him?'

'Not without a better reason. You're over-reacting, Livvy, distressing yourself like this.'

She had to give in gracefully. 'You're the doctor,' she said, because she was getting no help from him.

The top floor of the farm had been converted from a warren of attics into a well-appointed apartment when Maybelle Cramer had come home from America after her husband died. Livvy's parents had been struggling with the changeover of a farmhouse into a guesthouse. Most of the land was sold, but money was still needed, and Maybelle had provided.

She was in her sixties then. Behind her was a long and happy marriage, but everyone knew her here as Maybelle Murrin because there had always been Murrins at Sweet Orchard.

She was a lovely lady, everyone liked her, and until three years ago she had been almost as supple and quick-moving as her great-great-niece. But then a fall and a broken hip had crippled her. A tiny lift had been installed, and now she sat on a smoky-blue velvet chaise-longue, half a dozen newspapers and colour supplements strewn around her, and with the Captain well back in an armchair huffing and puffing over a hard-hitting article in one of them.

Schula, the cat that had scratched and then strolled off, leaving Mischa to take the blame, was stretched out on the back of the sofa. She was a bluepoint Siamese, with a pale creamy-grey body, mask, tail and paws of deep grey, and white cheeks very sharply etched.

She watched Livvy with brilliantly blue eyes, and Livvy put her face close to the cat's and murmured, 'Aren't you the wicked one? And it's no use crossing your eyes at me.'

Maybelle had brought her cats with her from America. Since then there had always been two Siamese here, and no shortage of folk remarking that Livvy could look like her pets.

So did Maybelle. The blue eyes were faded now, just as the pale gold hair had silvered. But she still had the fine bone structure, and she was fastidious to the point of fussiness. From a side table she took a cleansing tissue, and wiped the newsprint from her fingertips.

Henry looked over his newspaper to enquire, 'You saw that young man?'

'Yes.'

'I felt I'd met him somewhere.' Henry was fishing for information, but Livvy couldn't explain in here and she said, 'I'm expecting Andrew any time. I'm just going to get washed and changed.'

'Have a lovely time,' said Maybelle.

Livvy changed out of her paint-smeared clothes into dark blue velour trousers and a harebell-blue lambswool sweater. Skilfully made-up, her eyes looked huge, and she looked at herself in the bedroom mirror and wondered if she could influence a hard-headed journalist like

Corbin Radbrook enough to persuade him to leave Aunt Maysie alone.

She must appeal to him, sweet-talk him. She looked soft and sweet, with her translucent skin and dewy eyes. But it was the claw in the velvet paw, because if she was cornered she could scratch, although Andrew for one would never have believed it.

She and Andrew had been friendly from childhood and for the last year closer than friends, and that afternoon they drove out to look at a property that the estate agents he worked for had been asked to handle—a modern detached house that should sell easily. In the evening they ate at a pub that was under new management, testing that out. And all through their time together Livvy seemed to be her usual bright self.

Andrew brought her back to her own home just after ten o'clock. Their goodnight had been tender, and Andrew really was the dearest of men, although she had never once considered telling him what was haunting her.

The television was on in the small parlour, and all the doors into the hall were closed. Livvy went upstairs to the first floor, and then up the second flight to Maybelle's apartment. That was in darkness too, except for a rose-pink lamp that bathed the living-room in mellow light and cast a glow into the bedroom through a door that was kept ajar at night.

She stood for a while by the bedside, looking down with the protectiveness of a mother for a child. In deep, tranquil slumber, the old woman's face was almost un-lined, and the silver hair seemed fine as spun silk. She looked so fragile and so serene. If she was dreaming, they were gentle dreams.

Nothing like the nightmare and delirium that had fol-lowed her accident, when Livvy had watched over her day and night, terrified that anyone else might hear her raving about the hell of jealousy. Or catch the words that she had moaned at the height of her fever…'I killed Laurie…'

CHAPTER TWO

THOSE had been the darkest days of Livvy's life, changing her from a carefree girl into a lonely woman.

The death of her mother and father in a car crash had seemed like the end of her world. Such a terrible, unbelievable thing to happen. Friends had rallied round, of course, the house had seemed full of them day and night, and Maybelle and Livvy had clung together.

Maybelle had been the stronger of the two. She had held back the tears while Livvy wept; her pale set face had steadied Livvy, and on the day of the funeral they had stood together, walked together from the churchyard.

It was the last day that Maybelle walked anywhere with an unfaltering step. Maybe tears made her stumble, causing the hip fracture, and the heart attack followed. Or perhaps grief triggered a cardiac convulsion. She was found quickly on the floor of her apartment, a matter of minutes after the funeral party returned to the house, and for Livvy the horror went on.

Until then no one had realised that Maybelle's heart was so weak that there was no question of putting her on an operating table. At best, she would be a semi-cripple for the rest of her life. At worst, her life was drawing to an end. In hospital she was desperate to return home, but when they brought her back to her own bed there was a relapse. Her temperature soared and Livvy, haggard with exhaustion and despair, never left her side.

A nurse was in attendance, but that night Livvy had persuaded her to go to her room and snatch a little sleep.

Later she wondered if it had been chance that had left her alone with Aunt Maysie, or if she had had some premonition of what she was going to hear.

When Maybelle moaned, 'Oh, my love, my love,' she thought it had to be Edward, the husband whose photograph smiled across from the bedside table. She dabbed the old woman's flushed face with a cologne-soaked tissue and bent to kiss her, whispering through her own tears, 'Don't leave me. Don't go away.'

Maybelle was in a fevered coma, but now she echoed, 'Don't leave me, Laurie,' and her hand reached out, closing convulsively around Livvy's fingers. Livvy had no idea who Laurie could be, Aunt Maysie had never mentioned anyone of that name, but now she was reliving a passionate love-affair and nobody should be listening.

If Livvy could have moved away she would have done, but the grip on her hand held her tight, and she was filled with pity as the old woman became a girl again, tortured by jealousy. There must have been a scene of unbearable anguish. Maybelle's beautiful face was ravaged; her head thrashed to and fro on the pillow as she moaned and sobbed. Only a few words were audible, but a torrent of words must have been screaming in her burning brain, and Livvy tried to wake her.

Nothing reached her. She was in another place and another time—and then her eyes opened wide. Not seeing Livvy, seeing something that turned her to stone. Her lips hardly moved and she spoke in a flat, dead voice. 'I killed him. I killed Laurie.'

It was a hallucination, Livvy told herself. A delusion, a horror fantasy. Nothing mattered then but keeping Aunt Maysie alive, and when her hand slipped limply from Livvy's fingers Livvy stopped breathing. But

Maybelle was breathing still, deep in coma or sleep, but breathing.

When the nurse came in the following morning Maybelle opened her eyes and the nurse smiled. It was several days before Dr Aslett admitted that the crisis was over, and Livvy slept on a put-u-up beside Aunt Maysie's bed, never going out of earshot. The hotel was closed, Aunt Maysie was the only thing that mattered. And if the bad dreams came back Livvy had to be near to hush and comfort her.

There was no more delirium. Maybelle Murrin was weak, but her mind became stronger and clearer every day, unaffected by her fall or the fever. And she had, Livvy was sure, absolutely no recollection of regressing over half a century and seeing her lover die.

Because it had happened. Even while she was telling herself it had been a nightmare, Livvy had to know. The first afternoon Aunt Maysie left the house, carried downstairs and tucked up in the back of Henry's car to visit friends who were waiting for her with open arms, Livvy went into her apartment.

Maybelle was a hoarder. She had drawers full of mementoes, letters, photographs, most of them from her years in America; but there was no mention, as Livvy scanned feverishly, of anyone called Laurie.

Until she found the sketch at the bottom of the big cedarwood chest. It was pen-and-ink on a postcard, in a lilac-coloured envelope that also contained a faded photograph of a dozen or so young folk. 'Garden party at Red Mullions' was written on the back of the photograph.

Livvy looked hard at that, but it was the sketch that gripped her. She was kneeling in front of the chest, the contents piled carefully beside her so that she could re-place them in order. She was hating what she was doing, but now a real sickness came over her, griping her stomach muscles as she stared at the head-and-shoulders study of a young man, and a girl who was enough like herself to have been her sister. Except that the date was 1929 and the names beneath were Maybelle and Laurence.

After her own name Maybelle had written 'Charles'. Maybelle Charles. She must have thought then that it might become her name. She was trying it out, probably liking the look of it because the sketch was a love letter from the artist. The secret, intimate way they smiled at each other proved that, and this man had died that year and Aunt Maysie had said she killed him.

Until then Livvy hadn't known much about the case. She had heard about it; it was an old local tale, it belonged to the folklore of the area. She hadn't even got the name right. She had thought he was Leslie Charles, but he was not.

Laurence was printed clearly in the same black ink as the sketch. The girl who had been Aunt Maysie had written in an ink that had faded to lavender—the same ink and the same hand as the note on the back of the photograph. Her writing had changed over the years, but it was still recognisable.

Livvy began to repack the chest, putting everything back tidily, covering the envelope, burying and hiding it. Then she poured herself a stiff whisky from one of the Georgian decanters on Aunt Maysie's sideboard and sat with her head in her hands, blaming herself for not leaving well alone.

Schula had been a kitten then, clinging sharp-clawed to the pale blue velvet curtains. Livvy had unhooked her and held her, stroking the wriggling little body until the kitten had looked up into her face, eyes crossing in ecstasy.

Heaven protect me from falling in love, Livvy had thought, because love had driven Aunt Maysie mad. It had passed. She had become a serene, self-controlled woman, with nothing left of the wild, abandoned passion that must have torn her apart. She had buried that, like the sketch and the photograph, under all that had happened since.

Tonight she slept peacefully in the bedroom beyond the open door, and the dimmed rose-pink lamp stood on the cedar chest. No one had disturbed that since she had opened it herself, Livvy was sure. Although it was probably a copy of that photograph that had brought Corbin Radbrook here.

'Was there a photograph?' Livvy had asked. She could remember it vividly. And the sketch. It would be a disaster if a copy of that ever fell into his hands. But the sketch had to be a one-off, and some time when she was sure of being alone in here she would dig out that envelope and destroy it.

Schula trotted beside her as she went downstairs. The cats could pick up vibes like nobody's business.

Sonia and Henry were in the parlour watching television. There was a much larger drawing-room, used by the guests, but this was the 'family' room, and even when the hotel was closed this was where the 'family' gathered.

All the furniture in here was old and comfortable. The walls were pale green, and a faint perfume from a lustre bowl full of pot-pourri roses mingled with woodsmoke.

An open fire burned in the Victorian fireplace. Henry sat in his usual red leather wing-backed chair, and Sonia sat at one end of the sagging three-seater chesterfield. Everything was as it had been ever since Sonia and Daisy arrived, but now there was a time bomb ticking away, although only Livvy and the cats knew.

Sonia and Henry beamed at her, their smiles vanishing when they saw how grave she was.

Livvy said, 'That man this morning who wanted to see Miss Murrin—he didn't mean me. He meant Aunt Maysie.'

'Corbin Radbrook,' said Henry triumphantly. 'I remembered who he was.' He picked up a book that was lying at his feet and waggled it, and Livvy sat down on the end of the sofa, with Schula on her lap.

'Well, he came here because he's working on a TV script, something that happened in the twenties, when an artist——' she swallowed '—was killed. A Laurence Charles.'

'I've heard of him,' said the Captain cheerfully. 'What's it got to do with Maysie?'

'She lived here at the time. She might have met him. And he wanted to interview her. I don't think it's a good idea—he'd get her confused and agitated. He's a hardline journalist.'

The Captain gave a snort of laughter. 'I've never met the man yet who could confuse and agitate Maybelle!' He offered the book to Livvy. 'You read this. I've got another of his in my room, and they'll tell you something about him. He isn't going to upset a lady like Maybelle. It's only the wrong 'uns he gets rough with.'

Livvy took the book, gently easing the cat off her lap. 'Thanks, I could do with something to get me to sleep.'

'Oh, it won't do that,' said Henry, and she went up to her room, handling the book as gingerly as if it was booby-trapped. She did not want to read it. She did not want to take it to bed with her.

In the doorway she looked down at the Siamese and said, 'Off with you, I don't need you to hold my paw,' and Schula went up the next flight of stairs to settle for the night on her cushion in Maybelle's apartment.

In bed Livvy started reading, and soon wished she hadn't. *Unholy Trinity* was about three conmen, and how Corbin Radbrook had helped get their come-uppance. None of it reassured her. Nor did the photograph on the cover, and the few lines of biography that said he had trained as a lawyer. That could be why his interviews never missed a trick. There was no sign of weakness in the face. If he saw the chance of getting at the truth, how could anyone double-cross him, even if it had happened sixty years ago?

A third of the way through she shut the book with a snap, because she could take no more. He must be given no clues to follow. He must never suspect that Maybelle Murrin had been closer to Laurence Charles than that photograph at the garden party. They were not together on that. The man called Laurence had his arm round another girl almost in another group, and the girl called Maybelle was not looking his way.

Livvy dropped the book down by the side of her bed and flicked off her bedside lamp and tried to fall asleep. But she woke several times and remembered every time, so that it was ages before she could sleep again; and when she was due to get up she felt sluggish and heavy, and no match for what lay ahead. The book was still there. Of course it was, Corbin Radbrook was no mirage.

She got under the shower, shutting her eyes and raising her face as the water streamed down over her. She towelled her hair dry and put on enough make-up to hide the traces of a restless night. Everything had to seem normal when he arrived this afternoon.

Before then she had to warn Aunt Maysie, and she was dreading that because there seemed to be no way to even say Laurence Charles's name without striking at her ailing heart.

Livvy took up a cup of tea and went through the morning routine of helping her aunt select her outfit for the day. There were panic buttons in the apartment, unused so far, and when Livvy went up a second time, with breakfast tray, mail and newspaper, Maybelle was up and dressed, sitting at a small table by a window.

There was usually something for her in the post, and she opened an envelope with a pearl-handled paper-knife, then asked, 'What *did* that man want yesterday? The one Henry was telling me about.'

So there could be no soft approach. Henry would have told her Corbin Radbrook's profession, and Livvy had to come straight out with it. She tried to sound casual. 'He's writing something for TV about Laurence Charles.'

She went on placing the contents of the tray on the table, not looking directly at Aunt Maysie, but she saw that the hands opening the letter were still. 'He asked if he could talk to you,' she said, 'because you were both on a photograph in a newspaper, and he thought you might remember him.'

'Yes,' said Maybelle.

'I said I didn't think you could help much. It was so long ago, and it wasn't as though you'd really known him.'

'No,' said Maybelle. The light had gone out of her eyes; they were as dull as grey stones. 'What would this man want to ask about?'

Livvy poured more tea from the small pot. 'About him and his friends, I suppose.' She added milk to the cup and pulled a face. 'Between us two, I didn't like him very much. He seemed very pushy, so I wanted an excuse to say no. He's coming back this afternoon, and I wouldn't mind showing him the door.'

Maybelle scooped in her own sugar, stirring slowly and carefully. 'You do what you think best, dear, if you think he might be tiresome.'

'Leave it to me,' said Livvy, and she couldn't help adding, 'Are you all right?'

'Oh, yes,' said Maybelle, looking out at the leaden skies and shivering. 'It's winter coming on. I've always hated winter.'

Laurence Charles had died on a winter's night, Livvy remembered that now, and she knew that Maybelle was remembering.

She worked hard, finishing the bathroom and starting to strip paper from the walls of one of the bedrooms as the clock edged inexorably closer to three in the afternoon.

Sonia thought she was being too protective, keeping Maybelle from seeing Corbin Radbrook. 'What harm could it do, letting him ask her a few questions?' said Sonia. 'He looked gorgeous in that photograph. How was he in the flesh?'

'Overpowering,' said Livvy.

'Of course, it isn't really my business——' Sonia began.

And Livvy said sharply, 'That's right, it's not,' so that Sonia flounced off in a huff.

Upstairs Henry was discussing the TV programme with Maybelle. When Livvy went up she said gaily, 'Henry thinks it's a pity we're not entertaining Mr Radbrook. He thinks it would be good publicity for us.'

'I don't,' Livvy said flatly.

Maybelle said, 'Anyhow, there's nothing I can tell him. You'll deal with him, won't you?' The TV script was hot gossip. They could have talked of little else, but she had not been caught off guard again. She did not know how she had betrayed herself when the fever was on her, and she must have thought her shock this morning had gone unnoticed.

She was keeping her secret and her will-power was strong, but physically she was like fine china that could shatter at a touch.

'I'll deal with him,' said Livvy. The bull in the china shop, due here any time. If she could not persuade him to go away and stay away, that had to mean winning his confidence, even if she had to seduce the bloody man . . .

Sonia gave a wolf-whistle as Livvy came downstairs, and she asked, 'What time are we expecting him?'

'Now,' said Livvy.

She was wearing a cream polo-necked sweater and trousers and brown suede boots, and Sonia smirked, 'I didn't think you liked him.'

'I don't.'

'Well, he'll get the message when he sees you. He'll know you haven't gone to any trouble, just throwing on that old thing.' Sonia's sarcasm was blatant; the trousers and sweater were new, so it was easy to see that Livvy wanted to look her best.

He was punctual. At three o'clock Livvy saw his car coming, and she was opening the front door when it stopped. Stepping out to greet him should show that she was anxious to be as helpful as she could and had nothing to hide. She meant to walk right up smiling, but at the bottom of the shallow steps she stopped dead, because as he came striding towards her she was suddenly scared he was going to grab her.

She tensed, swaying back against the impact that never came, because when he did reach her he didn't touch her. But for a moment it was like coming up against him hard and close, having the breath crushed out of her, so that she gasped before she could say, 'Hello.'

'Everything all right?' he asked.

She still seemed to be swaying slightly. Now she made herself smile. 'Yes, and with you?'

'Couldn't be better.'

Livvy turned back into the house, saying, 'Do come in,' over her shoulder, although he was hardly likely to stay outside. She could hear him behind her as she led the way to the parlour. The fire was kept banked up in here and she poked it to stir a flame.

'Sit down,' she said. 'Can I get you a drink?'

He said, 'Later, perhaps,' so he thought there was going to be a later, and she didn't argue. She could have used some Dutch courage herself, but knocking it back alone would alert him that she was not as calm as she seemed.

So she sat on the sofa, trying to look relaxed, and Schula, who was not fooled, sidled up.

'I phoned my aunt's doctor yesterday,' she began chattily, 'and I told him what you told me. He isn't at all happy about it.'

'Another thing I was told about Siamese cats,' said Corbin Radbrook, 'they squint.' Schula, having managed to drape herself round Livvy's neck like a fur collar, was looking at him with perfectly focused eyes.

'Wrong again,' said Livvy. 'Most of them only go a little cross-eyed when they're under a lot of stress. Or it can be a look of love.' She peered up through her fall of hair, squinting horribly, 'Like this,' and he winced.

'Must be agony!'

'Not at all.' She lifted Schula off her shoulders, placing her on the floor. 'I was saying, any sort of excitement is bad for my aunt, and the doctor said he wouldn't be responsible for what might happen if she got distressed. I mentioned the man to her and she said she could hardly remember him, so she wouldn't be much use to you, but it was probably a murder, wasn't it? They did find him at the bottom of Blackrock Chine—and she could get upset if you brought the old days back to mind. The doctor really did say no.' She sighed, appealing tremulously, 'So *please* will you——'

He said drily, 'I saw Dr Aslett this morning,' and that shut her up. She must have mentioned the name, and he missed nothing. He took nothing on trust either, he had found out for himself if Maybelle Murrin was up to meeting him, and Livvy said coldly, 'That was very professional of you.'

'I am a professional.'

She did not doubt it. There was steel inside him, and she had been a fool to hope she could handle him. She said desperately, 'And she's all the family I've got and she obviously means more to me than she does to her doctor. What *did* he say?'

'That he thought she would enjoy being interviewed and he was sure I'd enjoy meeting her. Shall we ask her?'

'*No!*' The word was jerked out of her. 'All right, that's his opinion and he's a good friend and he's fond of Aunt Maysie—everybody is. But she is frail, and I'm scared for her most of the time, and I want to protect her from anything that could put the slightest strain on her heart. Because that *is* ailing, and he'd tell you that if you asked him.' She tried appealing again. 'There must be somebody else you can ask about the wretched man.'

'If there is, I haven't found them yet. You said you'd like to see this.' He took a folded paper out of his jacket and brought it across to sit with it beside her. 'This is the photograph.'

It was a photostat of the front page of the Island newspaper dated Saturday 16th December 1929. The headline said 'Mysterious Death of Local Artist', and over the photograph 'Laurence Charles with friends'.

Livvy took it, poring over it as if this was the first she had seen of it. The caption gave names including 'Miss Maybelle Murrin of Sweet Orchard Farm' and 'the dead artist'. Some of the other names Livvy knew—local names. But he was right, they had all gone. There couldn't be many left to remember.

'Did you know any of them?' he asked.

'Have a heart! How old do you think I am?'

He smiled. 'Sixteen?'

His face was close, the eyes were heavy-lidded. The mouth was hard and clean-cut—a mouth that might be cruel and that she had to keep smiling.

She smiled up at him. 'I'll settle for sixteen.' And he cupped her chin, fingers supporting, thumb lightly brushing her underlip.

'Now I'm not so sure,' he said.

He knew she was not sixteen, but as her eyes met his searching intensity she wondered wildly what he could see. She looked down, her lashes fanning long and silky on her cheeks. 'You're not easy to assess,' he said. 'We must get to know each other.'

'Must we?'

'Oh, yes.'

He sounded as though that decision was already made, and she enquired gaily, 'How do we go about that?'

'We could start with dinner tonight. And talk.'

Livvy thought fleetingly of Andrew, who was not going to like this, and then shock took over as Corbin Radbrook kissed her. She should have expected it. Her face was tilted, his fingers were stroking her jawline. But, when his mouth brushed hers, her gasp parted her lips and she went weak as water.

He knew how to kiss. Her experience of erotic kissing was limited, but this was a master's touch. It took a real effort not to respond and let the delicious sensations go on and on. It was hard to pull away and say, 'Do you feel we know each other any better for that?' sounding as if she had enjoyed it, but her heart was not hammering.

'It's a good beginning,' he said, as if he had enjoyed it too. But if she had slipped her hand under his jacket to rest where his heart should be, she was sure the beat would be steady. She was the shaken one, although she managed to sound amused.

'I'll pay for my own dinner tonight. I'd like a say about the menu.'

Talk would be on it, but she wouldn't. 'Trust me,' he said.

They were bantering like old friends and likely lovers. Livvy chattered and joked with Andrew, but not with this undercurrent of danger. Nor with such a sharpened sexual awareness. She dared not trust this man who could turn into her enemy, but she had to make him trust her. She got back to a safer subject. 'How old are *you*?'

'Thirty-two.'

She had thought mid-thirties or older. The lines would deepen when he frowned, furrowing the forehead and cutting between the brows, but smiling at her it was a young man's face.

Except for the eyes. They were those of a man who had seen more than most men do in a long lifetime. Complex and charismatic—it could be fascinating getting to know him, but she must always remember what she was hiding, and never let him get close to that. Nor too close to *her*, now that a kiss had shown her what effect he could have on her.

His arm was around her shoulders, but lightly, and she shouldn't shrug it off. Better let it stay, friendly and casual. 'Did you have any plans for before dinner?' she asked.

'I had hoped to see Maybelle Murrin.'

'She's resting. She does rest in the afternoon. Look, I could ask around for you and find out if there's anyone else.'

'You're really set against me talking to her? It wouldn't be third degree. Just a friendly chat over the teacups.'

She must not seem paranoid, so she said, 'Maybe, but there's no rush, is there? How do you go about getting a script together?'

'Are you interested?'

'Absolutely hooked. The highlight of my winter here is usually what colour to paint a wall. Now we've got our very own thriller about to hit the telly screen. Would you——' she gave him the full battery of fluttering lashes in comic entreaty '——be needing an assistant? Temporary, but very willing.'

'If that means you,' he said, 'you're on.'

It was like the beginning of an affair that nothing could stop, everything going fast and smoothly. He must have felt responsiveness in that kiss, although surely she hadn't responded? The surprise of it had nearly knocked her out, but she had kept her head.

'So brief me,' she said. 'Tell me how it goes.' She didn't have to pretend to be hanging on every word, because she was, and he put on an act for her, mimicking a fruity-voiced announcer.

'Tonight we go back to a mystery from the twenties. Almost forgotten now, the story had all the best thriller ingredients: sex, scandal, beautiful people and sudden death.

'In an artists' commune on the Isle of Wight, a young painter seemed to be on the threshold of a brilliant career. His name was Laurence Charles.'

In his own voice, 'A picture of Laurence.' He tapped the newspaper. 'A blow-up of this if nothing better turns up,' and Livvy thought of the sketch and what he would make of that, and went cold. 'We fix the character. He was twenty-five years old. He'd knocked about before he came here. A charmer, a Jack-the-lad. There are plenty of quotes about him in the press of the time.

'Then the locality. The house that was the centre of the commune has gone, but the area hasn't changed that much, and the building he lived in and used as his studio is a summer let now. It was Coastguard Cottage, now it's Halcyon Cottage.'

'Really?' So it was the place.

'Then we'll do a brief review of that year, more photos and films, finally settling down to the story and events leading up to his death, using actors, and as far as possible actual locations. We've got permission to use the cottage, make it look as near as we can to how it was.'

'You mean a reconstruction?' Of course. That was how TV told old tales.

'They call it faction. Fact as far as we know it, fiction to bring it to life.'

She didn't care what they called it, it was bringing it to life that worried her. 'With an actor as Laurence Charles?'

'Yes, and as this is all I've got to go on, I don't even know what he looked like. Dark or fair, what do you think?'

You couldn't tell from the newspaper reprint but, from the photograph in the cedar chest and the sketch, she would have thought fair. 'Sort of middling,' she said. 'Does it matter?'

'I'd like to know how he looked, how he sounded. If she only saw him at this garden party, he'd surely be fixed in her mind because of what happened afterwards.' He must never know what really happened afterwards.

'When will we be seeing all this?' she asked.

'From the script being finished to the filming starting, about twelve months.'

A year before the ghosts walked. She held down a shiver and asked, 'And it's really the cottage?'

'Shall we take a walk around it?' She did shiver then. 'No?' he said.

'All right—why not? I'll get a coat.'

As she reached the door, he said, 'Livvy.'

She turned her head. 'Yes?'

'Don't be long.'

She smiled. 'I'll run!' She almost did, getting up the stairs, grabbing a brown quilted jacket and a long cream scarf, wrapping herself in both, slipping on cream woollen gloves.

She wished she could have locked her bedroom door and stayed in there, but he would have come looking for her, and when she reached the top of the stairs he was standing in the hall, waiting.

When she was two steps from the bottom he held out his arms so that she had to move close and let them close around her. 'I missed you,' he said, and she didn't have time to say anything because Sonia came into the hall then, taking in the scene at a glance.

'Well, you soon changed your tune,' said Sonia.

Livvy almost broke free. 'This is Corbin Radbrook,' as if Sonia didn't know. 'Corbin, my friend Sonia Baines.'

'How do you do?' said Corbin Radbrook.

'Hello,' said Sonia. 'Is Livvy going to let you make a telly star of Aunt Maysie?'

'*No!*' said Livvy fiercely, and Sonia giggled.

'Well, from where I stand it doesn't look as if you're refusing him anything.'

Livvy laughed at that, although it was embarrassingly tactless, and outside the house Corbin asked, 'What's her role in your life?'

'She lives here. She helps me with the guests. We practically went to school together, but don't get carried away by what she said about me not being able to refuse you anything.'

'Good lord, no, that's a ridiculous notion.' She could feel the pressure of his fingers on her upper arm through the jacket and sweater, sensation radiating as it had from his mouth on hers, making her tingle all over.

She said, 'I'm glad you realise that.'

'Oh, I'm a great believer in not rushing things,' he said. 'I reckon we'll need at least another week before we reach the stage where neither of us can deny the other.'

CHAPTER THREE

Livvy felt the colour burning in her face. She would do her best to keep him beguiled and bewitched, but sex was out. Today, next week, ever. She said, 'Me, too. I'm a believer in not rushing things. Do we walk?'

Blackrock Chine was about two miles away, cutting in from the sea and rising high. Coastguard Cottage, facing the sea, had been in a state of disrepair when the artists had started arriving, but Laurence Charles had patched it up and made it his home and his studio for that last year of his life. It was lonely, set apart even from his workmates, who had mostly moved into barns and a tumbledown farmhouse scheduled for demolition.

Other houses had long since been built on the old farm property. When Livvy had come searching she had stopped at the cottage, red brick with white door and window-frames, read the name 'Halcyon Cottage' cut into a wooden plaque on the wall, and thought, this could be the place.

She had gone quickly. There had been somebody at the window, and she had not wanted anyone enquiring if they could help and who she was looking for.

Corbin said, 'We can get near to it by car.' He opened the door for her, and from the back the dog eyed her balefully.

'How about Luke?'

'He's waiting to meet you.'

'You did say meet, not eat? What big teeth he's got! He isn't a pretty boy, is he?' He wasn't snarling, but he was showing a good set of sharp teeth.

Corbin walked round to the driver's seat while Livvy was hesitating. As he got in, he shook his head at her. 'Lady, with your cross-eyed cats, you're in no position to get personal.'

'But my cats are beautiful.'

She acted affronted, and he said, 'I happen to think he is.'

'Then there must be something wrong with your eyesight or your taste.'

'No way. Not when I look at you.' He kissed her again, his lips swift and sensuous on her cheek, seeking her mouth until she jerked her head back, then he said, 'Is your friend Sonia on the lookout?'

'She doesn't often see me in the arms of strange men.'

'I'm glad to hear it. What did she mean by "you've changed your tune"?'

'She knew I was worried about Aunt Maysie being harassed.'

'Harassed?' The word jarred on him. 'What makes you think I'd harass her?'

Livvy shrugged. 'I read one of your books last night. You certainly did some harassing there.' Because they had all had plenty to hide, and she must not start him wondering if Aunt Maysie had. She chattered. 'We've a permanent guest, retired Merchant Navy captain, he'd got your book. He's always buying books or begging them, and he never throws any away. He's got shelves full, probably sacks full too in his cupboards.'

'He was the man I met outside yesterday morning?'

'Of course you did. *And* he recognised you. He gave me your book to read myself to sleep with.'

'Did I send you to sleep?' His eyebrows quirked.

'No, in fact you kept me awake.'

'Good,' he said. 'Because when I get you into bed that's what I hope to do.'

'We're going to read one of your books in bed?' Her face was blank with idiot innocence, and he sighed deeply.

'The girl's a fool,' he said, seeming to address the dog behind them. 'Beautiful, but a fool.' Livvy turned in her seat, facing Luke.

'Tell the man the girl could probably teach him a thing or two.' Like hell she could, except—heaven help her—about Laurence Charles.

'I'll look forward to that.' He turned the radio switch for music and she laughed, making herself sit back and relax.

It was not far and the silence between them seemed easy, as though it was enough just being together. If they had met in any other way she would have liked him a lot, with his humour and his strength and the sexual challenge that was exciting and frightening. And she must guard against that every inch of the way.

She knew the chine, of course, and the road they took. A field off the road that was a car park in the summer was empty now. A stile led to the footpath from which you could walk down to the cove or climb up on to the downs over the chine.

Released from the car, the dog ignored Livvy, loping along beside Corbin, who swung long legs over the stile. Then Luke went over, climbing up and flopping down, and Corbin held out a hand to help Livvy, although she could have cleared it as easily as he had.

Once their hands were linked, they stayed that way. He wore no gloves, and, as they walked the track with fingers laced, she was conscious again of the electricity that seemed to flow between them, warming her although the day was cold.

There was a keen wind blowing, the skies were grey, the autumn colours had faded from heather and bracken,

and the trees were bare. It was beautiful in summer here,
beautiful in its way in all seasons, but all she could think
about now was how lonely it was.

She said, for something to say, 'You've been to the
cottage?'

'Yes.'

'Have you been here long?'

'Since Wednesday. I wasted four days.'

'Huh?' She meant, how?

'Not looking you up sooner,' he told her.

She laughed. 'Are you Irish? You've certainly got a
touch of the blarney.'

'That is not blarney.' Corbin raised the hand he held
and peeled off her glove, slipping it into his pocket. Then
he kissed the palm of her hand and laced her fingers
into his own again, and she felt as naked and as vulnerable as though his hand was on her breast.

She could hardly hear what he was saying for the blood
drumming in her ears, but she walked on with him and
he was talking about the way it used to be. 'There was
an old empty house along the coast, and half a dozen
artists took it over. There were outhouses, barns. More
came—at one time there were forty of them.'

He looked at her to see if she knew this, and she said,
'That many?' She wondered if she could say, Please give
me my glove back, my fingers are freezing. They were
not, but she would have felt safer with her hands in her
own pockets.

Then the path wound upwards, and as they climbed
higher the wind grew stronger. By the time they had
rounded a bend from which you could see the house,
she was breathless. It must have changed completely, and
be no more the place it was than Aunt Maysie was the
girl she had been, but she did not want to go inside.

Blinds or shutters were closed behind the windows; it looked like a place with secrets. Livvy watched Corbin produce a key, and thought, that wouldn't be the same key and maybe this isn't the door. Although the door looked old under the white paint and there were two keyholes, the smaller one was a modern lock.

The door opened smoothly, the hinges were oiled, and beyond was utter darkness, and she thought crazily—what should I do if someone in there whispered, Maybelle?

She could not walk into the dark. If Corbin had not stepped ahead without her she might have clung to him, but he went in and the dog followed, and Livvy stood on the doorstep outside.

She heard his footsteps, heard him swear, bumping into something, and then he was opening the shutters and light was filtering in. Her first sight had to reassure her because it was so modern and ordinary. A typical summer-let cottage, carpeted in hard-duty carpet, with a three-piece suite in dark brown, a few chairs, a low table, and in the kitchen alcove a stripped pine table and bench seats.

A door probably led to a bathroom, and an open wooden staircase rose to a landing and more doors. She stepped in as Corbin unlatched the shutters at the second window. She said incredulously, 'You're going to film in here? There's nothing left. There's nothing the way it was.'

'But it was the place.' He went up the stairs, sitting on the top step. 'Come here,' he said, and she climbed slowly, letting him draw her down to sit beside him. 'Now,' he said, 'use your imagination. You do have an imagination?'

'I know what I'm seeing. What do you expect me to see?'

He said, 'It was run-down. It had been empty for years. The floor was flagstones, the plaster was peeling off the walls. But during that summer he'd whitewashed the walls and brought up wood to burn in an old black stove.' There was a Calor gas stove now.

Papers had been burned here. Livvy knew the scent of woodsmoke and she could imagine the smell of burning letters, how they would curl and the violet ink that Maybelle had used would darken before the papers crumbled into ashes.

He went on, 'Table and chairs, a horsehair sofa, rugs, a black sheepskin and one of those old rag mats. He worked mostly in oils, and he was working towards an exhibition. He had his easel beside that window, canvases stacked here and upstairs.'

'All this is how you think it was?' She looked at him, not down into the little room that had no character at all, and he said,

'No. All this I've read. A reporter from one of the nationals came down and described it.'

She said, 'Go on,' because she couldn't say, I don't want to know. I wish I knew nothing at all. I wish I'd never heard what she said that night.

For a while afterwards Maybelle's secret had obsessed Livvy. Then, like Maybelle, she had locked it away, but now they planned to recreate this room so that Laurence Charles could walk again in it.

As Corbin described it, she saw it, and the happenings that night, so far as he knew them.

The artist had been found at the bottom of the chine. He had fallen from the cliff edge, and whether it was an accident or whether there was a fight, nobody knew. There had been a struggle in the cottage, drawers pulled out, upturned, cupboards rifled, papers burned. And on the floor was the painting of a girl—paint stripper had been poured on it so that only the magnificent black hair was identifiable.

The Dark Lady. There were theories about her. There were jealous husbands and lovers in the area whose dark-haired women might have been posing for that study. Suggestions ranged from the wife of a baronet who sailed her own yacht into a nearby bay, to a Spanish dancer who was appearing on the mainland, but was often spotted on the ferry to the island. And a few others.

But everyone had alibis, there were no clues left in the cottage. It had rained hard that night, so there were no tracks on the cliff edge, and by the time another world war had come and gone the nine-days' wonder was forgotten.

Luke was snoring at the foot of the stairs, and when Livvy asked, 'Don't you feel you're stirring up old ghosts?' Corbin grinned.

'He doesn't. If there were ghosts here, his hair should be standing on end.'

'Perhaps the vibes don't get through all that fur. My cats would be hopping.'

'From your cats, I'd believe anything,' he said, 'but the cottage was lived in again and it's had a stream of holidaymakers for the past ten years. When I contacted the owners, they couldn't remember Laurence Charles. Nothing that can't be explained goes bump in here during the night.'

'So you say.'

'We could prove it. We could stay till morning.' Soon it would be dark, shadows were falling, and Livvy shot to her feet. 'We could use the settee which probably pulls out into a double bed, and you could have my coat, and Luke gives off a good body heat.'

She went down the stairs quickly. She thought he was only joking, but she had to get out of here. She was outside when he closed the shutters again, and Luke lumbered past her, then waited for Corbin, who locked the door behind him and said, 'Foiled again!'

She tried to laugh, but it didn't come, and he asked, 'What is it?' He held her shoulders, turning her towards him, and she didn't think there would ever come a time when she could meet his eyes while he looked at her like this. She closed her own eyes for a moment.

'I'm a fool. But I do have an imagination and sometimes it goes into overdrive. You can laugh, but I've got cat-sense sometimes when the vibes get me.'

'Not a bad thing to have. Cats are survivors. With nine lives apiece, something must be working for them.'

It was because he had made her see the past so clearly, but she couldn't go on like this. She said, 'Not often. Usually I'm a cool customer.'

'Flame-proof,' he said, 'you told me. I hoped it was only your feet.' He led her away, an arm around her, and kissed her, still walking, so that it was a brief brushing of lips, but she felt it to the ends of her toes. Where he was concerned, no part of her seemed flame-proof.

In the car again, he said, 'Now, where do I take you to dinner?'

'Where have you been eating?'

'Nowhere that does a silver service. Tonight we should go upmarket.'

'Ah, but will they let us in?' she said gaily. They were dressed casually, but she couldn't see anyone barring Corbin Radbrook, and he did a Humphrey Bogart impression, upper lip stiffened, lisping in sinister fashion, 'You name the place, sweetheart, and I'll guarantee the red carpet.'

She did a husky-voiced Lauren Bacall. 'I know this little place where all I have to do is put my lips together and whistle.'

'What happens then?'

'They all come rushing to take my order, of course.'

'Tonight they'd better rush off as soon as they've got it, because I want you to myself.'

In this mood of gaiety Livvy could almost forget that tomorrow her troubles would start. She said, 'Actually there isn't much open this side of the island this time of year, but I do know a pub with a restaurant where the food is quite good.'

'I'll settle for it,' he said, and she gave directions to the inn off the seafront that she had visited with Andrew last night.

'We'll bring you a doggy bag out,' she promised Luke, and went ahead into a 'country cottage' type bar with its sprinkling of customers. Last night she and Andrew had sat at a table in here with a darts team playing behind a mock wrought-iron room divider.

Now she headed for an open door marked 'Callie's Kitchen'. The new manageress greeted her with a smile and said, 'Nice to see you again so soon.'

Then she saw Corbin, and her welcoming smile was replaced by a smile that said Livvy seemed to be doing better all the time.

There was no one else in the restaurant, six tables were laid, with red cloths and red candles in white holders. They took seats in a corner, and Callie lit their candles and produced menus.

'The seafood's good,' said Livvy. Andrew had had that last night. She had had some sort of omelette, and she had been so worried about Corbin's arrival that the subtle flavour of herbs and spices had been wasted on her.

Things were no better tonight. She was just as anxious. But she was hungrier, and there was a contagious vitality in Corbin that made her feel brighter. This was no five-star eating place, but she was finding it very pleasant when she looked at the man facing her across the table.

She chose the seafood platter. He ordered ham and eggs and a T-bone steak, and Callie made a note like a woman who liked a hearty appetite in a paying customer. She brought the food and a bottle of white wine, then closed both the doors for them, into the kitchen and into the bar, so that they were alone with a candlelit dinner for two.

Livvy found herself staring at Corbin's plate. The steak was huge, and there was a generous slice of ham. He didn't look like an overeater. He seemed big-framed and hard-muscled with no fat at all, and he said, 'You were the one who offered to bring back his supper.'

'Is that for Luke?'

'It would have been a tin of dogfood and a handful of biscuits, but after your promise he'll be expecting something better.'

She joked, 'Do let me make a contribution. A scampi, perhaps?'

'This,' Corbin tapped the steak with his fork, 'is ample. Perhaps a little fish for the cats?'

'They wouldn't thank me. They're fussy eaters.'

'Next time we'll book at the Ritz. Do you come here often?'

'I was here last night.' She sipped her wine, letting the cold liquid trickle down her throat. 'Before that, I hadn't been here for ages. But it's just changed hands and we were trying it out.'

'You and a man?'

'Yes.'

'I never considered that you might be involved with somebody.' He sounded as though he had missed what should have been obvious. 'You answer to Miss Murrin, you wear no ring, but look at you—of course there had to be a man around. Special, is he?'

She said warmly, 'He's very nice.'

'That I can live with,' he murmured, and she thought, what a wishy-washy thing to say. Very nice! She would have said that about Henry. 'I hope you've got no long-term plans for him,' said Corbin.

'How about you?' she countered. 'Do you have somebody special?'

'I think so.' He was looking at her, meaning her, and she should be joking, do you say that to all the girls? But the cliché stuck in her throat, and this time she couldn't drag her eyes away.

It was a shattering moment, making sense of what she had always thought was romantic nonsense about eyes meeting across a crowded room. Recognising someone who might make the earth move and the mountains sing. And he was the last man she dared get involved with.

She said, 'You don't know me,' desperately playing it light.

'Tell me what I should know,' he replied, and she had to look away.

'There's not much to tell. I run the hotel. My mother and father were in a car crash three years ago. Since then there's just been me and Aunt Maysie. Although you could say Henry and Sonia are part of the family. And you? How did you get into your line of business?'

'My father was a lawyer, I trained in the law, practised for a while. Have you any idea how many cheats and liars there are in the world?'

He was so close to one of them that they could have kissed across the table. Livvy gave a very small shake of the head, because he seemed to be waiting for an answer. 'I was involved in one case,' he said, 'that I couldn't get out of my mind, even after it was over and done with. That started me off, writing about miscarriages of justice. Then unsolved cases, searching for the truth.'

'Do you always come up with the truth?' Of course he didn't. Not every time, and please God not this time.

'Of course not,' he said.

'What made you choose Laurence Charles? You wanted something that was almost forgotten, but there must have been hundreds of cases to choose from.'

'Pure chance. I rooted through old files and found an account of it.'

'And it clicked?' She snapped her fingers. 'Like that? And you came looking for the Dark Lady.'

'I came looking for you.'

This was getting out of hand, and she said, 'You asked me if he was special. His name's Andrew and he is.' Andrew was the man in her life and that was special, but right now she was using him to protect herself against Corbin.

'I must meet him. Eat up now,' he said, dismissing Andrew like closing a door on a gatecrasher.

'So long as you remember,' she said.

She had one of the best evenings of her life, crazy though that was, giving herself up to the pleasure of a companion who seemed a perfect match for her. They were on the same wavelength or as near as made no matter, relaxed as old friends. He made her laugh, and she spun tales for him because she was a lively talker herself.

Plates were taken away, fruit and a cheeseboard brought, and Livvy smiled at Callie and said, 'Thank you,' but really it was as though she and Corbin were alone, apart from the world. She was enjoying herself so much that when they got up to leave she was surprised to see two other tables occupied.

In the car park Luke waited in the car. The steak was wrapped in a load of paper napkins, but he caught the scent of it and pushed a shaggy head between them. 'Not in the car,' said Corbin, shoving the package under the seat and winding down the window. They were well fed and the smell was not so appetising. 'Excuse me.' He leaned across Livvy to open her window too, then sat back, lifting her hair and sniffing behind her ears appreciatively.

'That's better. What is it?'

'My perfume?' His lips tickled her ear and she laughed. 'Very exclusive. I doubt if you'll find another like it. I mixed it last week from the dregs of four bottles I'd nearly finished. A couple dated from last Christmas, and between them now they should last me till this Christmas. Actually they mingled quite nicely; they could have been revolting.'

In the dim light she could feel rather than see him, his face by hers, the lean, hard strength of him against her even through the thickness of clothes. And when Luke growled she thought, he doesn't trust me, and she was not sorry because it brought her back to reality.

Corbin said, 'We're keeping him from his supper.' He put the car into gear and they drove back to Sweet Orchard, hardly saying anything, and Livvy thought, I feel as if I've known you for ever. Perhaps tomorrow I'll tell you, perhaps you would understand.

Lights were on in the little family parlour and upstairs in Sonia's room. The top-storey windows glowed faintly pink from the night-lamp, so Aunt Maysie must be sleeping.

Livvy had let herself out of the car. As she looked up, Corbin came round and put out a hand to stroke her cheek and rest on her shoulder, and said, 'About Andrew——'

She heard herself say, 'Who?'

His touch and his nearness, and the feeling that he was going to kiss her again, had confused her, and she gave herself an impatient little shake. 'Forget I said that. Thank you and goodnight.'

'See you in the morning,' he called after her.

She called back without turning, 'Any time after ten.'

She went straight up to Maybelle's apartment. Maybelle seemed to be sleeping peacefully, but the cats woke and yawned and stretched on their separate cushions. 'It's all right, go to sleep,' she whispered, and neither of them followed her down, so tonight they sensed that she did not need comforting.

Nor did she want Sonia and the Captain asking where she had been and what she had been up to, with the man she had been so set against only hours before.

In her bedroom she turned on the radio, finding music you could dream by, and went languidly about undressing and getting tomorrow's clothes ready. The jeans and paint-splattered shirt wouldn't do, because she was taking up her new 'job' as Corbin's assistant. If he was working on the Madeleine Smith script he could probably use a typist, and if he was researching Laurence Charles then she had to be there.

She went slowly through her whole wardrobe, finally settling for a grey flannel skirt and a scarlet sweater, with red boots or red flatties. And a camel coat with a soft leather, camel-coloured Enny bag that was Aunt Maysie's last birthday present to her.

She was acting as if tomorrow was a special occasion, and her reflection in the mirror showed her bright-eyed and flushed as a child before a party. Or a girl before a date with a man who thrilled her.

She should not be looking like that, nor feeling this way. Corbin liked her, and he was a man who went after what he wanted. Up to a point he might be a giver, but he would always take more than he gave. He would be an experienced and passionate lover, but no one would hold him body and soul as Laurence Charles had once held Maybelle Murrin.

This was how it might have started for Maybelle and Laurence. Liking and wanting, turning into something that was a kind of loving. Then the jealousy and the pain and the raging climax of that night in the cottage.

Had he already been killed by then? Had they quarrelled in the rain, walking near the cliff edge? 'I killed Laurie,' Maybelle had said. Had the destruction in the cottage occurred before or after? When had she burnt her letters and defaced her rival's picture, and what did it matter? A girl had run back that night to this house and no one had seen her, and she had gone on to live another sixty years.

Livvy loved her. In some ways they were alike, and since the night of the fever Livvy had been terrified of losing her mind over a man. That was one of the reasons she was happy with Andrew, because with him she was never out of her depth. There was no risk of being swept away in a storm of passion with Andrew.

The colour had faded from her face. She was pale now, shivering a little, and she finished undressing, slipped on a bathrobe and went into the bathroom near to her bedroom and ran a hot bath.

That stopped the shivering. She soaked in the scented water, filling the small room with steam, and not getting out until she was relaxed and drowsy. She mopped herself dry and was reaching for her robe when there was a rapping on the door that made her sigh impatiently.

There were four more bathrooms in the house; who wanted this one? She called, 'I'm nearly through.'

'It's me!' bellowed Henry.

'I'd go along the corridor if I were you. This one's like a sauna.'

The door was heavy, he probably hadn't heard, and Livvy opened it a crack so that the steam billowed out. 'Want a word with you,' Henry called.

She came out then, tying the sash of her robe, and saw Corbin a little way behind him.

'About putting this young feller up for the night,' said Henry. 'We've been having a tot of rum together.'

Henry's rum was 120-proof Navy brew, so potentially lethal that he rarely produced it. Now his usually ruddy face was the colour of a fiery sunset and his eyes had almost vanished. Henry was certainly the worse for wear, and Livvy said severely, 'Well, you'd better get to bed.' She looked down the hall towards Corbin. 'And what were you doing in here? I thought we'd said goodnight.'

'Fair's fair, m'dear,' said Henry. 'I went out and asked him in. He was just driving off. I wanted to tell him how much I liked his books.'

'You could have done that without the rum,' said Livvy. A couple of glasses of wine was fine, but Henry's rum on top of it would blow any breathalyser, and she would have expected Corbin to have more sense. Unless he had banked on being found a bed here.

'My fault,' Henry apologised.

'All right,' said Livvy, 'but it is only for tonight. Where's Luke? I don't want the cats coming down and meeting him.'

Luke had been fed and was bedded in the car, Corbin told her, and she opened a door and switched on a light. 'You can use this room. I'll bring you some bedclothes.' When she came back minutes later, arms filled with sheets and blankets, Henry had vanished and Corbin stood by the window, although it was too dark a night to see much out there. This was a good-sized room, and he stood quietly, but he seemed to fill it. Livvy felt his presence like a physical touch, as if the air between them was electrified.

She began to make up the bed, and he said, 'Thank you.'

'I didn't have much choice. I wouldn't put anyone behind a wheel who'd been on Henry's rum.'

'It's strong stuff.' He looked and sounded sober, but having agreed that he could stay she went on briskly, talking and tucking in the sheets.

'You could have asked Henry for some pyjamas, mine wouldn't fit you.'

'I don't use them.'

She shut that image out of her mind and said, 'And it's understood that you keep to your own room.' She had left her bedroom door open, and Henry would have gone there first. Corbin knew where she slept and he could be thinking of joining her.

'Understood,' he said. He hadn't moved from the window. 'Although I'd give years of my life to keep you with me tonight, and I speak as a man who enjoys living.'

She was looking at him across the bed and she wondered wildly if she could bargain. Herself—if he would leave Maybelle alone. But if they made love she could end up burning up, and she said, 'I don't jump into beds on a first date.'

That was true, she didn't jump into any beds but her own, and he said, 'Neither do I, I never have,' and his eyes were steady on her. 'I could make an exception in your case because you are exceptional, but we've all the time in the world.'

She said, 'Yes, we have,' but he was coming to her and he mustn't touch her. She whirled towards the door, and the girdle of her bathrobe, the end of which she had tucked under with the blankets, was jerked undone and her robe flew wide open.

Beneath, she was naked, and she gave a strangled shriek and grabbed the gaping edges. 'Fair's fair, m'dear,' said Corbin. 'Although who says life has to be fair?'

'Forget you saw that.' She held the robe together with one hand, and looped the trailing girdle with the other.

'Impossible,' he said. 'It's a memory I shall treasure.'

Livvy was laughing as she ran out of the room and down the corridor into her own bedroom. She hoped he didn't think that that had happened on purpose, that she had been deliberately provocative. She was glad nobody had seen her rushing half naked from his room, and that nobody knew how easy it would have been to have gone on laughing and stayed.

CHAPTER FOUR

THE HOWLING woke Livvy. She sat in the darkness and listened. It had to be Luke, and if he kept this up he would be rousing the household. The luminous dial of her travelling clock said a few minutes past six, so morning was not far away, but dawn hadn't broken yet and somebody had to shut the wretched animal up.

Corbin, of course. She switched on the bedside lamp, blinking against the sudden brightness as she rolled out of bed and groped for a robe, although now she was decorously covered in serviceable pyjamas.

As she slipped out of her room, Corbin came through his door, dressing in a hurry, pulling on a sweater. 'Sorry about this,' he said. 'I'll go down and walk him.'

She yawned. 'Thanks.'

'May I stay for breakfast?'

'Help yourself.'

She went back into her bedroom, and soon the howling stopped, although they wouldn't be walking far because the rain was beating on the window-pane. Now she was awake, she might as well go down and make coffee. And if Luke was loose there was always the question of the cats.

She got into jeans and a sweater and came out of her room into a silent house. No one else seemed to have been disturbed. The only light down here Corbin must have switched on when he'd reached the stairs.

In the kitchen she filled the kettle and spooned instant coffee into a couple of mugs. She'd told him to help himself to breakfast, but he would have to find the kitchen first. While she waited for the kettle to boil she went to the front door and walked out into what looked like being the start of a foul-weather day.

Even when her eyes grew accustomed to it she could see no further than the forecourt, and if he had taken a torch from his car there was no sign of it. 'Helloo!' she shouted.

'Helloo!' came back like an echo.

'Come on in! You'll catch your death, both of you!'

She was used to looking out for everyone in this house, but if ever there was a man who could look after himself it was Corbin Radbrook. When he strode up through pouring rain she said, 'How far does that dog need to go? Can't he see it's chucking it down?'

Luke seemed to be grinning, with his fur sleek and dripping, and the idea of Corbin catching his death of cold was ridiculous.

Livvy stood at the top of the steps. 'So you don't care about it raining,' she said, 'and neither does Luke, but he's got to be rubbed down, and I'd like him in and out of the house before the cats get up.'

She led the way down the hall and into the kitchen. She opened the door of the Aga and poked between the bars, shaking the ash through the red coals, then she took a towel from the cupboard. 'You both look as if you could use this.'

In the middle of the room Luke was shaking himself vigorously. Corbin bent down and began to towel him, looking up at her as she poured hot water into the coffee-mugs and enquiring, 'Doesn't anyone ever tell you to stay in out of the rain? You look like a half-drowned kitten.'

She was almost as wet as they were. When she touched her hair she could feel the rain on her fingers. She shook her head, as Luke had done, sending her hair swirling, then did a quick shrug-and-shake. 'It hasn't had time to soak in with me, it's all on the surface.'

'You do talk some rubbish,' he said, 'but I can't think of anyone I'd rather have with my morning coffee.'

She thought, I could learn to like having you here, and she joked, 'You don't have anything with your coffee, you take it straight.' She carried the two mugs to the table and sat down with one before her and watched him give the dog a final rub. After which, Luke flopped in front of the fire.

Corbin came to the table. 'Where did you find him?' she asked.

The dog was no breed she recognised. 'An animal rescue centre,' said Corbin. 'He was a stray. Probably thrown out because he was growing too big—and he hadn't half finished then.'

Luke's tail thumped lazily and Livvy said, 'He did all right. Do you take him everywhere?'

'When I'm abroad he stays with friends. Otherwise, yes. Where are the cats, by the way?'

'In Aunt Maysie's apartment, on the top floor.' The kitchen door was shut, but she must get Luke out before Schula appeared, and even Mischa might turn aggressive at finding a dog in the kitchen. 'They don't often come down while it's dark.'

There was still darkness outside the windows, but it was cosy sitting here. They talked as easily as they had last night, so that time passed, and Livvy made more coffee, and when the door opened she could hardly believe they had been here for over an hour.

But she was not as surprised as Sonia was. Walking along the passage, Sonia had heard Livvy laughing, and wondered what Henry was on about so early in the morning that was so amusing.

When she opened the door and saw Corbin holding Livvy's hand, telling her something that had her in helpless giggles, she stared as she had yesterday afternoon when she'd caught Livvy in his arms at the bottom of the stairs.

What had happened since then Sonia could only imagine, and it was not at all what she would have expected from Livvy. She was shocked rigid, and when Corbin said, 'Good morning,' she could hardly bring herself to answer.

Livvy said, 'It's never that time,' and that didn't help.

Corbin said, 'Come on, old boy,' and Luke lurched to his feet and loped out, following him.

'Well!' said Sonia.

Under Livvy's amused glance she bridled. 'I know it's none of my business, it's your life and your house. But he is a stranger, you can't know that much about him except that he must have knocked around. He's something all right, but I wouldn't have thought you'd have been carrying on like this. Not you.'

'Calm down,' said Livvy. 'There's been no carrying on. Henry brought Corbin in last night and poured out *the* rum. Then he had an attack of conscience and asked me to put Corbin up. Corbin had his own room, the dog slept in the car, and we met down here this morning when the dog started howling. I wonder you didn't hear it. No? Well, that's what happened.'

Livvy had no make-up on, not even a touch of blusher or mascara—and, even if she had fallen so hard that she was sleeping with the man within hours, she surely wouldn't be facing him like this this morning? Even her hair looked unbrushed, and although Sonia rarely used make-up herself these days she probably would if she ever fell in love again.

'Sorry,' she mumbled, 'only it was a shock. And yesterday, when you were in the hall with your arms round each other, I didn't know what to make of that either.'

'Don't make too much of it,' said Livvy, and she had to take her own advice. Being with Corbin had its marvellous moments, and letting him make love to her could be a dream come true. But some time, at some stage, the dream might change into a nightmare.

'You look washed out this morning,' said Sonia. 'You never drank that awful rum?'

'Would I be looking even this bright if I had?' Livvy shuddered, pulling a face, and as Corbin walked back into the kitchen she added thoughtfully, 'It didn't have much effect on you, did it, the Captain's rum? Strong men have keeled over on that and been out for twenty-four hours, but you were sober last night and healthy this morning, so how did you manage it?'

'I watched him down his first measure, and when it glazed his eyes I went slow on mine.'

'Didn't he notice?'

'He went on pouring, he's a generous host, but I got most of it back in the decanter. He got up several times to get books down.'

Corbin could have refused. But then Henry would not have offered him a bed here, where he was near Livvy and, possibly, near Maybelle Murrin.

'Well, I think it's funny,' said Sonia, and Livvy realised that she herself was frowning.

She smiled and lied, 'I was thinking, thank goodness you didn't pour it in the potted palm, or that could have been flat on its face this morning!' She stood up. 'Give me a few minutes and I'll get you some breakfast before you go.'

'Thank you,' said Corbin. A dark stubble of beard and moustache shadowed his jaw. She hadn't noticed it while they were laughing and talking, but suddenly it seemed to make him look older again.

Sonia asked him, 'Who was this man you're here to write about? What did really happen to him?' as Livvy left them.

Usually Sonia dashed down to get a cup of coffee and rushed right back to Daisy, but this morning she was staying to talk to Corbin. And why not? There was nothing that Sonia could say that could matter, but in the few minutes Livvy had been away Henry had come downstairs.

His complexion was less ruddy this morning and he was taking his coffee black, but sitting at the table with Corbin and Sonia he looked cheerful enough. As Livvy came into the kitchen he said, 'I'm sure Livvy will agree, won't you, m'dear—we can put Corbin up here, can't we?'

Corbin's expression was amused, and she asked, 'Whose idea was this?'

'Mine,' said Henry promptly. 'I'd like another man about the house.'

She said, 'We're closed. I'm in the middle of giving the place a face-lift.' She was painting and papering, one room at a time, and Sonia and Henry began to protest together.

Sonia was saying there was always a spare room, and washing bedclothes and cooking for just one extra would hardly be noticed. Henry, who had obviously enjoyed last night's session, launched into what a coup it would be to have a well-known TV writer working at Sweet Orchard. Good publicity for the place when the series was televised. Something to put in the brochures.

That nearly made Livvy laugh hysterically. This could end in publicity of the very worst kind and wipe the smile off Henry's face for good, but a lot of coffee on an empty stomach seemed to have made her light-headed. 'Besides,' Henry finished, 'don't tell us you couldn't be using the money.'

She looked at Corbin, and he said, 'Of course I'd like to stay here.'

And because her reasons against him couldn't be told she had to say, 'All right, we'll see how it goes for a day or two.'

It went like clockwork after that. Livvy cooked breakfast, and left Henry and Corbin eating toast and marmalade while she took Aunt Maysie's early morning cup of tea up.

The cats greeted her in the big living-room, and she said, 'I don't like to tell you who our new lodger is, but he's bigger than both of you put together.'

Maybelle was sitting up in bed, awake and waiting. 'Who is that, dear?' she enquired.

Livvy said, 'I'm talking about a dog. Belonging to somebody Henry wants us to put up because he fancies having another man about the house.'

She put the scalding hot tea on the bedside table before she went on, ever so casually, 'That writer, that Corbin Radbrook.'

But Maybelle reached for the cup with a steady hand and said, 'So it looks as if I will be talking to him.'

'You don't need to if you don't want to.'

'I don't see how I can be of much help, but I don't mind seeing him.'

Livvy said, 'OK, we'll let him up some time. What are you going to wear today?' Then, like every morning for nearly three years, she took the clothes Maybelle wanted from the closet and laid them to hand.

Sonia and Henry were delighted. The winter months were usually dull, and they saw Corbin Radbrook as someone who would help to fill the empty house and the empty days. Last night he had told Henry that some TV folk might be coming down soon, and Henry was all for opening Sweet Orchard to them. Livvy surely would not turn down business like that?

'And don't fret yourself about Maybelle,' said Henry. 'She'll be in her element yarning about the old days.'

Livvy could have told him that it would not be a gentle stroll down memory lane for Maybelle. She looked at their happy faces and thought, if I could only make you understand the ordeal you're setting up for her.

But she could tell no one. Certainly not Corbin. She couldn't know what use he would make of that information, and she must guard against the chemistry between them that could so easily cloud her judgement.

She was back at her desk, dealing with a booking for next year that had arrived this morning, when Sonia came in and said, 'Why don't you let him work in here? It doesn't get used much these months, but it is a sort of study, isn't it? And it's warm.'

Most of the rooms upstairs were unheated when the guesthouse was closed to visitors, and the office *would* be a good room for a writer. With a patio window opening into a small conservatory and out into the gardens, Corbin could have the dog in here with him.

'Don't make him too comfortable,' Livvy said. 'I don't want him settling in.'

Sonia smirked. 'Wouldn't Andrew like it?'

'Why should Andrew mind? And I wasn't the one who suggested him moving in, either.'

'You didn't say no,' said Sonia.

They were waiting when he came. After the midday meal was cleared away Henry sat in his window alcove, telescope trained on the road along which the car should travel, shouting from the top of the stairs, 'Here he is!'

Livvy had gone back into her office. If Corbin was going to move into here she had some clearing out to do, but she heard Sonia's scurrying footsteps crossing the hall.

She went on emptying a couple of drawers in her desk, transferring the contents to the other drawers. Letting him use the office was not such a bad idea. It meant she would have access to his papers and be able to learn what he was finding out.

He came into the room with Henry and Sonia and Daisy, and Sonia said, 'It's all right, isn't it, Livvy? Corbin can use the office?'

'I suppose so,' Livvy said, and as he thanked her she told him, 'It was Sonia's idea.'

When he smiled at Sonia, she squirmed with delight.

'This will be ideal. I do appreciate your thoughtfulness,' said Corbin, and Livvy watched him chatting them up. The charm might be part of his stock-in-trade, but he very soon had three fans here.

Sonia wanted to feed him, although he had had lunch. Henry was enjoying the man-to-man rapport. Daisy asked, 'Do you really write stories?'

'I do,' he said, 'and I can tell stories too.'

His cases were carried upstairs. A typewriter, a tape-recorder, and another caseful of papers and files were brought into the office, and when they were alone Livvy opened two drawers in the desk and said, 'I've cleared these for you. Oh, and if you want Luke with you, keep the doors shut.'

He closed the hall door and she knew he was going to take her in his arms. She found herself moving around, keeping out of reach; then he stood still, and so did she—with half the room between them. 'If you're staying here,' she said, 'remember what I said last night.'

'I remember, but what's wrong in being close? I only want to hold you.' The pull between them was so strong that her every nerve seemed to be clenched and aching from the strain of holding back, and her voice sounded bright and brittle.

'Not here. Sonia could come dashing in with some nourishing soup whether you want it or not, and she's confused enough as it is. She thinks you're a fast worker, but she hopes I'm saying no.'

'I am and you are.'

'And we're keeping it that way.'

Corbin laughed. 'Right, all right, so it's down to work.' He put most of the papers and files in the top drawer, explaining, 'That's Madeleine, I'm working on her in the mornings. These,' placing a much thinner file on the desk, 'are Laurence, and the rest of the day is for him.'

He didn't have much yet, but that was why he was here, to fatten up the file, and Livvy said eagerly, 'I can be in on that? You will let me help you?'

'You can do anything you like with me with my fullest co-operation.' He leered and she laughed, and he took a typewritten sheet out of the folder. 'We can start on this right now. When can I see Miss Murrin?'

When Livvy had brought down Aunt Maysie's lunch tray Aunt Maysie had said, 'If that young man does turn up this afternoon, I might as well get it over with.'

Now Livvy said, 'Suppose I asked you, as a favour, not to bother her?'

'Why?' His eyes had that piercing quality again. No warmth, just a quick, cool scrutiny, and she knew that Henry would have talked about Maybelle last night and said she was as bright as a button, probably that she was looking forward to meeting Corbin. The more desperate Livvy sounded, the more suspicious Corbin would become.

She was twisting her hands nervously, but she managed to sound as if she was admitting that her attitude was stupid. 'I suppose I'm fussing. I feel I'm in charge here and I've got to look after everybody. Calling you and Luke in out of the rain this morning was going over the top, wasn't it? And Maybelle is old and I worry about her.'

'I can understand that,' he said quietly. 'But who looks out for you? Andrew?'

'He would.' Of course he would. 'But I don't need looking out for, I can look out for myself. I'll go up now and see if she's resting. If she isn't, I'll ask her if she'll see you, but please don't overtire her.'

'I promise,' he said. 'Anyhow, you'll be there, claws at the ready.' And she made a pretend swipe, fingers flexed like a cat's paw, and went out of the room, smiling.

Most of the time with Corbin she seemed to be smiling, and yet there had never been a time when she had been so scared. Maybe when she had thought Maybelle was dying, but nobody had smiled then. Now the smiles were hiding such turmoil that she might start laughing and end sobbing, with Corbin transformed again into an inquisitor watching her with cold eyes, asking, why?

Perhaps soon the worst would be over. All Maybelle had to do was say that yes, she was here when Laurence Charles and his friends had their commune of artists, but what she could remember of them could be told in a few minutes. Livvy would work with him, moving heaven and earth to sabotage anything that might link Maybelle with Laurence. But Maybelle herself was surely the only danger. What had been so close a secret all those years ago should be beyond discovery now, if Maybelle kept her head and the strain did not break her.

No one would have guessed, as she sat on her chaise-longue greeting Corbin with a ravishing smile. She was still a remarkably pretty woman, and he stood for a few moments as if he could hardly believe his eyes. Even with fifty years between them her flirtatiousness was not grotesque, it was charming when she said, 'Livvy told me a young man wanted to see me, but she didn't tell me how handsome he was. Although Henry did say he was famous.'

'Henry flatters me,' said Corbin.

'That's Henry's way.'

Henry was usually brusquely outspoken, but she smiled with Corbin at a shared joke. 'Do sit down.' He took a chair facing her and Livvy sat on the very end of the chaise-longue, arms folded and gripping her elbows, trying not to look apprehensive.

'You're here to write about——' Maybelle made a fluttering little gesture as if she was striving to pluck a name out of the air.

'Laurence Charles,' Corbin prompted.

'Yes, of course.' Livvy knew it was a name Maybelle would never forget, and wondered how long it was since she had consciously spoken it aloud. Right now she hadn't been able to say it. 'My, that was a long time ago,' she said. 'I was even younger than you.' She looked fondly at Livvy. 'So very long ago.'

'Do you remember him at all?' Corbin asked.

'I did see him once.'

Again he prompted, 'At a garden party?'

Livvy had told her that he had seen the photograph, and now she said, 'That's right, that was when I saw him. From what I recall he was a good-looking young man, he seemed to laugh a lot. We all did—or perhaps I'm imagining that, but I'm sure the sun was shining and it was a lovely day.'

'Did you talk to him?'

'Only a few words. The artists and the islanders didn't have much to do with each other. But I do remember that the garden party was for charity, something for the church.' Maybelle leaned forward, smiling as if this was a game. 'What do you want me to tell you?'

'Could you describe him for me?'

'Well, as far as I can remember, he was tall, fair, as I've said, good-looking. If you're writing about him, you probably know more about him than I do. What have you found out?'

'Not much,' said Corbin. 'What the papers printed at the time. He had parents alive then. There were no others, that was his family. After sixty years, finding anybody who knew him is an uphill job, and I've only just started.

'I've advertised and talked to the local press. There'll be something in the *Midweek News* tomorrow asking for anyone who has any sort of information. What I'd like to do is get hold of some of his work. Did you see any of it?'

'No,' she said.

'He was preparing for an exhibition. There were a number of paintings in the cottage, something might turn up. Not the Dark Lady—that was destroyed. It seems no one even bothered taking a photograph of that.'

Livvy wished she could put her arms around the frail old body. 'There must have been talk about the Dark Lady afterwards. Do you remember that?' Corbin asked.

Maybelle said brightly, 'I didn't hear any of that, because I wasn't here. I was in America. It was the year I got married.'

Laurence Charles had died the night before Maybelle Murrin sailed. Livvy knew the dates, but Corbin did not, and he had no cause to check. He didn't think she would need an alibi. He said, 'What I'd like you to do, if you will, is help me cover that year. Any background, any photographs, what it was like here then. Would you do that?'

'Of course I will. It was my last year in England for nearly forty years. It will make me feel young again.'

Livvy said with frantic gaiety, 'He's taking me on as an assistant, so you can tell me—I'll interview you.'

'I can talk to you any time,' said Maybelle, sounding as though she was enjoying herself. 'But not many handsome men want to listen to me.'

She thought she could fool him with flattery, and perhaps she could, so long as he never suspected what she was doing. But she was fooling herself if she believed that his easygoing manner was more than skin-deep. He had a mind like a razor and they didn't come any tougher, and Livvy sat a little longer, while Maybelle talked about how life was when she was a girl and he listened attentively.

Then he said, 'I'm under orders not to outstay my welcome. May I come again?'

'I hope you will,' said Maybelle, and Livvy went with him to the top of the stairs.

She said, 'Thank you for keeping it fairly short.'

'It was long enough. She'd have talked on, but she was tiring herself.'

'Was she?'

Maybelle had seemed gay and lively describing her youth, when the sun always seemed to be shining. Livvy thought her performance was flawless, but Corbin said, 'It was a strain for her, I felt that,' and she felt a jerk of panic when he went on, 'I don't know why.'

'I told you—because she's old and her heart plays up. I'll see you downstairs. I'd better get back to her.'

He did have the knack of sensing more than people were telling, and heaven help Livvy if he ever used it on her. If he stripped away her layers of pretence she would be revealed as a double-crossing cheat.

'What a charming man,' said Maybelle when Livvy walked back into the room.

'Very charming,' said Livvy coolly. 'Not my type, but he has his fans. Sonia's drooling over him, and Henry. And Daisy's thinking about it.'

'But you don't like him?'

Maybelle found this amazing, and Livvy said, 'He'd sell his own grandmother for a good story.'

Maybelle's eyebrows arched. 'You seem to know him very well.'

'I'm learning,' said Livvy. 'While he's here he's hoping to seduce me in his spare time.'

So he was, and she was encouraging him. But if Maybelle thought he was pestering Livvy she would not approve of that, and now she was looking anxious.

'Well, it's a cheek, isn't it?' said Livvy. 'I've told him about Andrew, but he's the sort that you could be wearing a wedding ring and it would make no difference. You know, meeting someone like him really makes me appreciate Andrew.'

It was awful that she was lying. Corbin had pushed Andrew out of her mind so that even while she went on talking about Andrew she was wondering if—when it was all over and Corbin had gone—she could ever go back to Andrew. It was awful, because that was not how she wanted it to be.

Maybelle asked quietly, 'Why are you telling me this? I'm aware of Andrew's good qualities.'

'Yes, well,' said Livvy, 'it's just that I don't think Corbin's got many of them. Now, shouldn't you be resting, or shall I send Henry up and he can tell you why he made me take in a lodger when I wanted to shut up shop?'

All this must have been upsetting for Maybelle. Livvy was not happy about leaving her alone just yet. Henry would be quick off the mark if she should need her panic pills, and she said, 'Oh, ask Henry to come up, I don't feel tired,' and as Livvy turned to go she said, 'Those old photographs he was asking about, I don't think I've got anything like that.'

'I didn't think you had,' said Livvy as Henry appeared in the doorway.

'All right if I come in?'

Corbin was in the conservatory leading off the office. There were plants in here, fuchsias, geraniums, and assorted cuttings sitting the winter out. It was pleasant and warm, but he was standing looking across the bleak, rain-swept lawn, his back to Livvy. 'All right?' he said, without turning. Her step was almost soundless, she was shoeless again, and she said, 'How did you know it was me?'

'I'll always know if it's you,' he said, and she had to go to him and stand beside him as he asked again, 'All right, is she?'

'You were right, she was feeling tired.' She looked out into the rain too until he turned her towards him.

'She must have been very like you. When I first saw her, I thought, sixty years ago she could have been Livvy.'

As if she needed reminding not to fall as Maybelle had for Laurence, as she could fall for him. She said lightly, 'There's a family likeness, I suppose, and she's just said you're a charmer, so perhaps we sometimes think alike.'

He laughed at that, and that afternoon he went over the items he had on file with her. Livvy read the copies of the old newspaper cuttings, correspondence with the owner of the cottage, local editors and librarians. There were notes of contacts who were looking out for paintings for him, and after the appeal in tomorrow's papers somebody might turn up who could tell them more.

They sat side by side at her rosewood desk, fingers brushed, and Corbin smiled at her, smoothing the hair from her forehead when it flopped, making no effort at all to keep his hands off her. And she flirted as far as she dared.

Luke was brought in from the van to join them. He was a travelling dog, used to strange rooms. He sniffed around this one, growling softly at Livvy before he settled down.

'It's the cat in you,' said Corbin. 'I make allowances for it, but he'll take a little longer.'

Outside it rained all day, but inside everything seemed sweetness and light. Maybelle must have been worried, but no one would have known; and when evening came she and Henry settled down to watch an old movie in her apartment.

Livvy shut the door on them and the cats and went downstairs. When she had left the parlour to run up to Aunt Maybelle, Corbin had been starting a bedtime story for Daisy about a favourite toy, a woollen owl. She was spellbound as he described the spreading wings with Daisy perched on top, off on an adventure to one of the stars, and Livvy thought how ironic it was that he should be making up fairy-tales while the real-life drama was being kept from him.

When she returned, the scene in the parlour had hardly changed, except that where Daisy had been sitting on the sofa beside him it was now Sonia, listening with the same rapt delight. 'We're not still with Oozy the owl?' said Livvy, irritated without knowing why.

Sonia chortled, 'He knows *everybody*! He knows——' She reeled off names from TV and journalism. She had asked him if he had ever met Terry Wogan, and from then on he had been telling her behind-the-scenes gossip that she was loving.

Livvy could hardly remember Sonia being so animated. If Corbin stayed on Sonia could perk up, but she must not get too much of a crush on him. Not just because he was attracted to Livvy, in the long run nothing could come of that, but because it just would not do. They were chalk and cheese, in no way right for each other.

The front doorbell rang and Luke started barking. 'Now who——' Livvy began, and at once remembered. When Andrew had kissed her goodnight on Sunday night, he had said, 'See you Tuesday,' but she had had so much on her mind, it was a wonder she hadn't forgotten her own name. Now she scrambled to her feet and said, 'That'll be Andrew—I'll get it.'

She pulled Andrew in out of the rain as soon as she opened the door, babbling, 'Isn't it horrible, we won't be going anywhere in this, will we? And there's somebody here I want you to meet.'

She held his hand, as they had walked for miles together over the years, and she knew that it was only affection she felt for him, because this was nothing like the charge of electricity that seemed to come from Corbin's touch. They entered the room, still hand in hand, and Corbin looked across, eyes raking them. When he stood up he was much taller than Andrew, or perhaps it was just that he was the dominant personality.

'Andrew Becker,' said Livvy. 'I've told you about Andrew.'

'Indeed you have,' Corbin murmured.

'Corbin Radbrook,' said Livvy. 'He's working on a TV script and he's spending a few days here.'

Andrew was surprised, then intrigued, listening to Corbin talking about his work. They sat chatting, first about Laurence Charles and then about other things— Andrew's job, properties on the Island. Anything and everything, with Corbin always courteous, always charming, so that Sonia was enthralled and Andrew quite forgot he had come here expecting to spend the evening alone with Livvy.

Andrew recommended a place around there where the food was good to Corbin, and told Livvy, 'We might go along there, how about Sunday evening?'

'Why don't we make up a foursome?' suggested Corbin. 'I have to go to the mainland during the weekend, but I'll be back on Sunday. We could all go out together.'

'That would be smashing. Henry would babysit,' said Sonia eagerly, and when Andrew said goodnight to Livvy he smiled about that.

They stood by the front door in the hall and he said, 'I've never seen our Sonia so keen on fixing up a baby-sitter. She couldn't keep her eyes off him—he could be just what she needs.'

'Or the last thing she needs,' Livvy snapped. 'She could easily get hurt, and he couldn't be tougher, even if he does have nice manners when it suits him.' She opened the door. 'Drive carefully,' she said. Since her parents' accident she always found herself saying this in the rain. She watched the car go, and she couldn't believe that Andrew was boneheaded enough to think that Corbin and Sonia would ever make a compatible couple.

As she turned into the hall she saw Corbin at the top of the stairs. They had all said goodnight. Sonia had gone to her room and Corbin had taken Luke up to his. Now it seemed he had been waiting for Andrew to leave, standing in the shadows up there. He hadn't had long to wait, and she asked, 'Is Luke safe, because I have to let the cats out for a few minutes?'

'The door's shut.'

'What do you want?' She walked up the stairs towards him.

'To say goodnight to you without onlookers.'

'If you don't like them, why did you fix for us all to go out together on Sunday?'

She reached him where he lounged against the wall, arms folded, and he drawled, 'I wasn't having you going alone with Andrew.' He stayed where he was as she went on up the stairs to the top floor apartment. Maybelle slept, the cats followed Livvy out when she whispered their names, and Corbin joined the small procession into the kitchen, where she opened the back door.

Pouring milk into two saucers, she told him, 'Andrew thinks you could be just what Sonia needs.'

'Not me,' said Corbin promptly. 'I'm what you need, and vice versa. I was glad to see you'd forgotten he was coming tonight.'

Livvy put the saucers down for the cats, who had sauntered out, found it was raining and belted back, and muttered, 'I did not.'

But he went on cheerfully. 'He's a habit, that's all. Like cleaning your teeth. How long have you known him?'

'Always.' So she had. She was used to Andrew and very fond of him. She said gaily, 'He gave me a lovely clockwork duck for my fifth birthday.'

Corbin grinned. 'What did he give you for your last, the key to go with it?'

'Very funny!' The cats lapped up the milk. 'Anything else I can get you?' she teased. 'Like a cup of cocoa?'

'From you I'd take it. And that could be what Emile said when Madeleine handed it over and said, "Trust me."'

He was joking, but Livvy suddenly felt sick. He shouldn't be trusting her, and how could he be so perceptive about everything else and not know that? She must be his blind spot, and she could only pray that he never would see her clearly.

'So no cocoa,' she said brightly. 'You two finished?' The cats had. 'So come on.' She switched off lights as they went back upstairs, and at the foot of the second staircase she said, 'Goodnight,' and added, 'You really don't wear pyjamas?' Corbin shook his head. 'Well, please wear a towel to the bathroom, because there are ladies present, and I do mean Sonia and Daisy.'

She was fooling, of course, and he grinned, 'Don't worry, I keep a robe handy in case of fire, but there isn't going to be a fire tonight, is there?'

He reached for her hand, running a fingertip over the blue veins in her wrist, and it was like a little flame that could have raged out of control if Livvy had not pulled away. She ran up the second staircase, calling over her shoulder, 'No fire, and no walking, with or without a robe!'

When she reached the top of the stairs and looked down at him, he said gently, 'Goodnight, my pretty.'

And she heard herself answer, 'Goodnight, my love.'

She stayed in Maybelle's apartment for a while, huddled and silent in a deep armchair. It had to be just the chemistry of sex. She was desperately attracted to him, it was fierce infatuation, but it was not and it must not be love.

CHAPTER FIVE

HENRY picked up the papers in the hall next morning on his way to the breakfast table, and entered the kitchen reading the caption under a front-page picture of Corbin. 'Corbin Radbrook, well-known crime writer, is on the island hoping to solve an old mystery. See page three.'

He spread out the pages on the table, and Sonia squealed, 'Let me see!' and rushed round and began to read out loud. So did Henry, not always the same bits.

'Mystery of Blackrock Chine,' the headline said. 'How did Laurence Charles die?' There was a picture of the chine in summer, although surely it should have been winter. A couple of paragraphs about Corbin, his TV credits and that he was researching for a programme that would be filmed here next year. There was a fairly full account of the story 'Who was the Dark Lady?'. And it also said that he wanted to meet anyone who could remember Laurence Charles or the artists' commune. Any of Charles' work, any photographs, please get in touch with Corbin Radbrook c/o the *Midweek News*.

Livvy stood back as Henry and Sonia gleefully read out snippets. Sonia was getting a real kick out of this, and Henry's regret was that he had arrived on the scene forty years too late. 'Maybelle will want to see it,' he said. 'I'll take it up to her.'

'I will,' said Livvy, and wondered if this appeal would revive local memories, even after all these years. She shivered and knew that Corbin noticed, and made herself smile at him and say, 'The ghosts are walking.'

Sonia first giggled, then remembered Daisy and said, 'Not really there aren't any ghosts.' But there are, thought Livvy. The ghost of the girl who could have been me sixty years ago is close to me now. And she couldn't look at Corbin.

Maybelle asked for the paper when Livvy took in her first cup of tea, and read it while Livvy moved around the room. She looked pale and tired, and Livvy asked, 'How did you sleep?'

'Not too well,' she replied.

And she didn't protest when Livvy said, 'Have breakfast in bed. Get up when you feel like it.'

Downstairs, Livvy told them, 'She's tired this morning; no more interviews for a while.' But Maybelle ate her breakfast, and by mid-morning she was up and dressed and writing letters to friends.

Livvy went back to what she had been doing before Corbin erupted into her life, stripping paper from a bedroom wall. In the office Corbin was at work, with Daisy as a constant interruption until Sonia, for once, laid down the law. The office door must stay shut because if Luke got out there could be a fight with the cats.

Livvy heard this going on in the hall and Daisy wailing, 'They might not fight, they might be friends!'

'Don't go in there.' Sonia sounded stern. 'Be a good girl now—he's working, he mustn't be bothered.'

But Sonia wasn't applying that to herself. The guestroom where Livvy was was near the top of the stairs. With the door open she heard Sonia's footsteps crossing the hall every time, and then the tap on the office door and Sonia saying, 'Coffee?'

Over breakfast Corbin had said he operated on black coffee when he was working. Sonia had taken that to mean a cup every thirty minutes, Livvy reckoned, and at last she went down to the kitchen and filled a flask.

Sonia was sitting at the kitchen table, with a magazine open at a page of hairstyles. Without looking up, she asked, 'Do you think something like that would suit me?'

When they were students Sonia's hair had been short and flipped, and normally Livvy would have been pleased to find her taking an interest in her appearance again. But it was all because of Corbin, and that was dead risky. 'It's pretty,' Livvy conceded. 'It would suit you.'

Sonia saw the flask. 'Who's that for?'

'Corbin,' said Livvy. 'He's got enough in there to last till lunch time.'

'Mummy's been taking him coffee,' piped Daisy.

And Sonia said, 'Shall I take it?'

'No.' Livvy held on to the flask, sounding sharper than she'd intended, and Sonia looked down at the magazine again.

'I'll get it done for Sunday,' she decided. 'I'm really looking forward to Sunday.'

Livvy went into the garden towards the conservatory door into the study, because she needed a breather in the open air. She was fuming with frustration. As if there weren't enough complications without Sonia falling for Corbin! Warning her wouldn't help, she wouldn't listen to advice. She was infatuated, and she was going to be hurt again.

Overnight the rain had stopped and the temperature had dropped. The frozen grass of the lawn crunched under Livvy's bare feet, and she cooled off so rapidly that she was glad to step into the conservatory. Luke growled, lying beside Corbin, and Corbin said, 'I don't think it's the cat in you, after all. I think he's jealous.'

She had felt like growling and snapping at Sonia, and maybe that meant she was becoming possessive about

Corbin. She said, 'That's silly,' scolding herself. 'Coffee,' she said. 'A flask of it. With all the interruptions, you'll never finish off Madeleine.'

She put it down on the desk, beside his typewriter and the last half-empty cup, and leaned across to look at the photostat of a letter. The crabbed writing was criss-crossed like a puzzle and the signature was 'Mimi'. She asked, 'Madeleine?'

'Yes. Copies, of course. The originals were used in evidence, and when they were taken out of the archives a hundred years later her perfume still lingered.'

That must have been a shock for whoever had opened the box. Livvy gasped, 'It must have been strong stuff!'

'Madeleine fancied the rough stuff,' he grinned, and breathed deeply against her hair. 'On the subject of scent, you've changed yours this morning.'

She was wearing none, except for the scent of clean skin and hair and a minimum of make-up; although her hands were sticky and there were splashes down her jeans. She sat on the edge of the desk, swinging a long leg. 'What you're getting,' she said, 'is a whiff of wallpaper remover and stale paste.'

'Interesting. Daisy's wearing your brand.'

So Daisy had been at her dressing-table again, and she rolled her eyes ceilingwards. 'Daisy's a little monkey. She keeps out of the guestrooms because she knows what would happen if she didn't, but she's in and out of my room all the time.'

Corbin leaned back in his seat, watching her swinging foot. 'I wish you'd wear shoes.'

'Why? My feet are doing you no harm.'

'They're disturbing feet.'

She put on a look of mock concern. 'Do you have a foot fetish?'

'Only for your feet.'

'Sorry about that, I wouldn't disturb you for the world. I'll take them away.'

'Mind how they go,' he said. 'They're beautiful, I don't want them getting hurt.'

Livvy wished she could accept his protectiveness and his arms around her, instead of fooling all the time. 'Ah, well,' she said, 'back to the striptease, three coats of paper I'm dealing with.' And, as she opened the door into the hall, 'I wonder what we'll get from the article in the *News*.'

'We can but hope,' he said.

She hoped for nothing, and she nearly got her wish. By Friday the *Midweek News* had produced some old photographs, although none of Laurence Charles, and four very senior citizens who said they remembered him. Two were in their seventies who had been teenagers at the time, one in his eighties and one in her nineties.

Livvy went with Corbin to meet them, and saw the skill with which he established a rapport that had them liking and trusting him. He let them ramble on, but what it came down to in the end was that they were here at the time of the artists' commune, they might have met Laurence Charles, and they remembered the fuss and the rumours that had followed his death.

The Dark Lady was a gypsy dancer, the ninety-year-old said, revelling in her role as star of the old people's home talking to a man from the telly; and as Livvy and Corbin drove back to Sweet Orchard afterwards he said, 'I'd give my eye teeth to meet somebody who actually saw that bloody picture before it was destroyed.'

Maybelle had seen it, but it had been painted in secret. No one had come forward at the time, it was unlikely anyone would now. 'You never know your luck,' Livvy said tritely, and he took a hand from the driving wheel to cover her hand briefly.

'Oh, yes, I do,' he said. 'You're my luck and my love. They don't always come together, but when they do they're unbeatable.'

She was neither luck nor love, and smiling back was cheating. So was saying, 'All that and I can type too. I'll get the tapes done while you're away.'

The interviews had been taped, and she might as well type as wallpaper over the weekend. Corbin put her down at home, leaving almost immediately to drive to Yarmouth and join sailing friends who were taking him to the mainland. Livvy stood by the car as he lifted in the smaller of his cases, and Luke bounded on to a seat. She said, 'Goodbye, see you Sunday.'

'Indeed you will.'

He kissed her, and from the steps leading into the house Sonia and Daisy chorused, 'Byee!' waving vigorously.

Corbin called goodbye as he drove away, and Livvy stood with her hands in her pockets, still feeling his hands on her shoulders and the sensuous pressure of his mouth on hers. She had wanted to say, Don't go. It was as if this was a rehearsal for the time when he would go and never come back. Life would be safer without him, but in some ways she would miss him.

Sonia waited by the front door to ask, 'Who are they, these friends he's meeting?'

'I don't know.'

'What's he going over for?'

'I don't know that, either.'

'You don't know much, do you?' Sonia decided that Livvy was not being tight-lipped. She hadn't asked and Corbin hadn't told her, but he had kissed her goodbye, and Sonia couldn't resist pointing out, 'He could be going to a girlfriend. Or a wife.'

'I don't think so,' said Livvy as Sonia walked beside her down the hall.

'He's famous, isn't he?' said Sonia. 'If he did have a wife we'd have heard about that, but there can't be many women who'd say "no".' And she mused wistfully, 'I wonder who he'll be sleeping with tonight?'

Rage blazed in Livvy, so that she could have turned on Sonia like a tiger, and she bit the soft inner surface of her lip to keep in the angry words.

'Anyhow,' said Sonia, 'it's going to be dull here without him.'

Although he was only away for a couple of days, it made all the difference. It seemed so quiet without the rattle of his typewriter, odd being able to leave doors open without checking on the cats, and looking for Luke. The buzz seemed to have gone out of everything. Even Daisy was grizzling more than usual, and although Sonia read bedtime stories to her they didn't go down half as well as Corbin's tale in which Daisy and her toys were playing the lead.

Livvy had expected to feel easier when he was out of the house, but she couldn't keep him out of her mind, and most of the time she didn't try. There was his voice on the tapes she was painstakingly transcribing; and sometimes she would rewind and listen again because listening to him made her smile.

She had plenty to do, but the hours dragged. She had always enjoyed the winter months when this was just a family house, but now without Corbin everything seemed bogged down, as if there was no urgency or excitement any more.

She had finished typing from the tapes and was making the final corrections on the manuscript when Sonia and Daisy returned from the hairdressers. Sonia had had her hair cut and curled, and Daisy's was a fair copy. They tripped into the office like a music hall act, and Livvy obligingly clapped her hands because it was such an improvement for Sonia, and Daisy looked cute. 'Terrific,' she told them. 'You both look sensational.'

'I got a new dress too,' said Sonia.

The table was booked for seven o'clock Sunday evening, but after six there was still no sign of Corbin. Sonia had been getting ready for hours. Her new dress was loose-fitting but brighter, in multicoloured jersey, than the clothes she usually wore, and she was putting on make-up for the first time in years.

Daisy was sulking. She did not want to be left behind while her mother went out with Livvy, and they could tuck her up in bed all they liked, but she wasn't going to sleep until her mother got back.

Although Sonia was out of practice she enjoyed applying the make-up, and after a session of putting it on and rubbing it off and trying again she felt confident enough to go into Livvy's room and ask, 'How do I look?'

'Like your old self,' said Livvy, and it was almost true. When Andrew arrived her confidence got another boost, because he said, without any prompting, that she looked stunning. 'You've done something to your hair, haven't you?'

Sonia and Livvy pulled faces at each other. 'Just a little something,' said Livvy.

'Is Corbin back?' asked Andrew. 'Or am I going to have two gorgeous girls to myself?' and Sonia pulled another kind of face.

'He isn't back yet. It would be awful if he wasn't coming.'

'He'll be here,' said Livvy confidently.

'How do you know?' Andrew asked. 'He's cutting it fine.'

'Because he said he would.' Her assurance puzzled him. She was wearing a black velvet skirt, black tights and patent pumps and a black mohair sweater dotted with seed pearls that looked like snowflakes or tears. Her silver hair fell smooth and shining. Her eyes glowed, and faint colour warmed her high cheekbones. She looked so beautiful that he would have taken her in his arms if Sonia and Daisy and Henry had not been looking on, just to remind her and reassure himself that she was his.

Within minutes they heard the car arrive and Corbin was calling, 'I'll be right with you,' as he hurried down the hall and up the stairs.

Sonia babbled happily, 'Well, I wasn't as sure as you that he was going to turn up. He could have had a better offer. Or an accident.'

I would have known, thought Livvy. I knew he was coming, just as I know that we're going to have a lovely evening.

She was learning to shut out her fears of the future and make the best of what was happening right now. It wouldn't last, it couldn't, this was borrowed time, but tonight she was so glad to see him again, and when he came into the parlour where they were waiting his eyes held hers and nobody else mattered.

They took Andrew's car. Livvy sat in the front passenger seat, Sonia and Corbin in the back, but Livvy was so overwhelmingly aware of Corbin that they could have been alone together.

He had been staying with friends, he said, and dealing with some business affairs. He complimented Sonia on her hairstyle and she went into a rambling account of Daisy at the beauty salon selecting the style for them both. Andrew talked property, and usually it was interesting enough hearing what was coming up for sale and what had just been sold and for how much. But tonight their voices flowed over Livvy, who had been gazing out of the window and now looked back over her shoulder.

Corbin smiled at her. Down the side of the seat, out of sight of the others, their hands touched. Her fingers curled in his and her breath exhaled in a soft, contented sigh. She relaxed, not saying much. Neither did he, except for the occasional remark that kept the other two talking.

Livvy and Corbin communicated by touch. A quick squeeze that said, 'You're here, I'm here, everything is all right now.' Palm rubbed palm, fingertips played. They ran through a whole range of sensory signals, sometimes jokey, sometimes erotic, in the twenty minutes it took to reach their destination. And as the car drew up Livvy reluctantly let go.

That was how the evening went, with other things not always what they seemed. Sonia and Andrew were in great form, and a lot of that was due to Corbin. He laughed at their jokes, he asked questions they could answer. He kept them happy. But all the froth and bubble was on the surface. Beneath, deeper waters flowed.

It was as if Livvy and Corbin were lovers, so that every word that passed between them was like a caress. Livvy could not understand how Andrew and Sonia were missing what was going on under their eyes, when it seemed to her she was giving herself away all the time. So was he, she would have thought, every time he looked at her. But Sonia and Andrew and everyone else here could have been on another dimension, were on another wavelength, enjoying themselves and suspecting nothing.

There was dancing. During the summer a live group played. Tonight it was piped music, but most of the diners took a turn on the floor. Some danced close, some gyrated apart, and Livvy danced with Andrew and Corbin with Sonia.

Andrew was a competent dancer. Livvy had always enjoyed dancing with him, but when they changed partners and she was in Corbin's arms she was not dancing at all. She was floating. The others seemed like shadows, as though there was only this man, with the handsome, hawklike face and the beautiful, burning eyes.

She said dreamily, 'I've had the oddest feeling all evening that we're alone.'

'We are,' he said. 'There is no one else.' And Livvy wished the dance would go on for ever.

But it ended, and so did her evening. When the house came into sight, as they drove towards it, almost every window seemed illuminated, and Sonia gave a strangled shriek. 'Is it on *fire*?'

The glow was steady, with no flickering, and the wrong colour for fire, and Corbin said quickly, 'No, it's just lights on.'

'There are a lot of lights,' Livvy gulped as she spoke, because something must be wrong, and Andrew put his foot down on the accelerator, turning into the drive with squealing tyres and drawing up in the forecourt to a screech of brakes.

Almost before he stopped, Sonia had tumbled out of the back seat and Livvy had jumped out of the front, and the four of them arrived at the house together. Livvy was digging in her purse for her key, but the door was unlocked and Sonia ran into the hall, screaming, 'My baby, where's my baby?'

The house was still, except for Luke barking from the direction of the kitchen. Pieces of a crashed jardinière and a mess of potted leaves and peat were scattered about the hall. Until then Livvy's reaction had been that

Maybelle must have been taken ill, but this looked like vandals, a break-in. She didn't know what to think as she ran for the stairs with Sonia still screaming behind her.

Henry appeared on the landing, puce-faced, white beard and scanty hair bristling, and Livvy called, 'What's happened?' 'Where's my baby?' Sonia screamed.

'Your baby,' roared Henry, 'is under the bed!'

Somehow Corbin had passed them both and reached Henry, who turned to him as though he was the relieving cavalry. 'Thank heaven you're back, my boy. She's under Livvy's bed, her mother can get her out, I can't.'

'What's she doing there?' demanded Sonia, and Henry struggled to control himself, and finally spluttered, 'Gone to earth. It's been like a battlefield here.'

The chaos in the hall was worse than Livvy had realised in that first fleeting glance. The hall table had been swept clear, a chair overturned.

Daisy must had thrown a king-size tantrum and, although it had been hard on Henry, and she really was spoiled rotten, Livvy wanted to laugh. Mostly through relief, but the idea of Daisy, pursued by Henry as she smashed and crashed her way around the house, finally diving under a bed where he couldn't reach her, had a comic side.

She said, 'You mean Daisy ran amok?' and saw that Corbin was hiding a grin.

'Daisy,' said Henry, still shaking with rage as they all trooped into Livvy's room, 'let the dog out. She knew you'd left him in the kitchen, and she knows about the cats. We told her not to go downstairs, and she must have crept down quiet as a mouse, and the cats were in the hall and she let the dog out.'

'Where are the cats?' Livvy was concerned again. Going by his bark, Luke was in fine fettle, but what about the cats?

'In Maybelle's apartment,' said Henry. 'He couldn't catch them, but it was a madhouse. They were everywhere, up and down the stairs, knocking things flying. I managed to shut the door between them when he went after Schula into the parlour and she got out first.'

He slowed down. From then on the panic had been over, and it had been a mopping-up operation. 'Maybelle was up there,' he jerked his head towards the top floor landing, 'so I got her back into her room and poured her a brandy and she called the cats up. Then I got Luke back in the kitchen and poured myself a rum. And then I went after Daisy.'

He looked and sounded apoplectic. Sonia said defensively, 'How do you know Daisy let him out?' although Livvy didn't doubt it for a minute.

'Because she was down there,' Henry spluttered. 'Because when I did find her, she said, "Mummy shouldn't have gone and left me. She'll be sorry now."' You could almost see the steam coming out of his ears. 'If I could have got her out,' growled Henry, 'she'd have been sorrier!' and Sonia went pale.

The worst that would have happened to Daisy would have been a roaring telling-off and a speedy return to her bed, but she wasn't risking it, and Livvy couldn't blame her. She must have known that she had gone too far. 'I went all over the house looking for her.' So that was why so many lights were on. 'Then I crawled around, looking under the beds.' Livvy could understand why Henry was furious; it was very undignified for a retired sea captain. He glared at Sonia. 'Don't ask me to baby-sit again. Next time she could be burning the house down!'

He stamped off to his room and Andrew said, 'I'd better be going.' He grinned. 'Poor Henry—I hope you get her out.'

Sonia said, 'She's frightened. She's only a baby.' She went down on her knees beside Livvy's bed and cooed, 'Daisy, it's Mummy. Be a good girl now, come out.' There was no reply and Sonia whispered hoarsely, 'Can you hear her breathing? You don't think she's suffocated?'

'Of course not,' said Livvy. 'There's plenty of air.'

'I'll have to pull her.' Sonia's head and shoulders vanished under the bed and then she stuck. After a moment of wriggling, she squirmed back. 'I can't do it. Livvy, would you?'

The bed was against the wall and Daisy was curled up in the corner like a dormouse. Her thumb was in her mouth and she appeared to be sleeping peacefully. Livvy eased her out gently and Sonia cradled her head, crooning, 'Oh, she's asleep,' although Daisy's eyelids were twitching. 'I'll get her to bed.'

She carried her into their room and tucked her up. Daisy's small angel face was rosy against the white pillow, and Sonia said, 'I suppose I shouldn't have left her.'

'Don't let her hear you say that,' Corbin advised from the doorway.

'She can't hear me, she's asleep,' said Sonia.

'Not a chance,' he replied cheerfully. 'She knew that if she kept her eyes shut she'd just be put to bed, and she hopes in the morning everybody will have forgotten about it. Even Henry.'

'He's mad at her now.' Livvy laughed. 'I'd better check on Aunt Maysie and the cats.'

'I'll check on Luke. See you downstairs afterwards?'

'All right,' she said.

It was a while before she could join him, because although Maybelle was in bed the lights were on and she was waiting to hear about Livvy's evening and talk about Daisy. Maybelle had not found it amusing watching poor Henry caught up in a flying circus of cat versus dog, while she hung on to the top-floor banisters, unable to help. Nothing had been hurt. The cats sat on their cushions looking smug, and Luke hadn't caught them, so he hadn't even been scratched. But the jardinière was in pieces, and it hadn't done Henry's blood pressure any good, and somebody must talk to Sonia about Daisy.

'I will,' Livvy promised, 'in the morning.' She sat on the side of Maybelle's bed and said, 'We had a lovely time.' She went through the menu and she described the room. 'Sort of stately home stuff: panelled walls and oil paintings, a long gallery with tables round and dancing. It was lovely. We all enjoyed ourselves.'

'Has Andrew gone home?' asked Maybelle.

'Of course.'

'Where's Corbin?'

'Downstairs.'

'Waiting for you?'

'I am going down again, yes.' When Maybelle smiled, she said, 'Is there anything else you want?'

'Turn the lights out for me.'

Most of the lights in the house were out now, and the entrance hall was cleared and tidied. Broken pieces had been removed and debris swept up, the rest put in order. The parlour door was open, and Livvy went towards it. Corbin was sitting by the fire, and she asked, 'Did you do all this?' although she knew he had because there was nobody else.

'Sorry about the breakages,' he said. 'I'll replace them.'

'That could have been the cats.'

'Luke's the one who moves like a bulldozer.'

In here, with the firelight and with side lamps burning, the glow was mellow. Livvy stared at the child's toy that waddled towards her—a clockwork dog, black spots on white and a wide grin—and asked, 'What on earth is that?'

'It's your birthday present.'

'What?'

'Andrew brought you a duck, I brought you a dog. I was there. As long as you can remember I've been around. You had a birthday party.'

She sat on the rug in front of the fire, feet tucked beneath her. The toy continued its jerky progress into the wall, tipped over and lay there whirring. She said, 'Yes.'

'My folk had an apartment in Freshwater Bay. We were always there for the holidays. Your birthday is the twentieth of July.'

'Who told you?'

Anyone could have told him, but he said, 'I came, I always came,' and she wished she had known him all her life, because that was how it felt.

He took gifts from a bag beside his chair. A wooden-jointed doll for her sixth birthday, a tub of jelly babies for her seventh. 'You had a sweet tooth then,' he said.

'I still have.'

'I know,' he said, as if he knew everything there was to know about her.

There was a brush and a mirror and a comb, a child's set with bluebirds painted on it. He said, 'Your hair tangled when we walked along the coast. You walked barefoot and your hair streamed out in the wind.'

'We used to do that?'

'Not alone. There were always others then. I was all of sixteen, you were just a kid. You always tagged along, you were a pushy youngster. Smart, but too young for me.'

She could almost see him, head and shoulders taller than the other boys of his age, and smarter than any of them, and she brushed her hair with the child's brush and said, 'I looked forward to the holidays when you came. I liked the summer best, when we could swim and climb the cliffs.'

It was crazy, but they really did seem to be reliving memories as the presents came out of the bag, one for every year; and from her seventeenth birthday the gifts made her gasp. From then on they were beautiful and pricey. 'It was dawning on me,' said Corbin, 'that you were special. We were just good friends, but I liked coming here, seeing you and talking to you. Some of the things that happened, you were the only one I could tell.'

Livvy buried her face in a cashmere sweater the blue of her eyes, and said, 'I took such care of this. I washed it very carefully because I wanted it to last for ever.'

There were antique ear-rings, amethysts set in gold filigree, and for the next year a matching bracelet. There was a leather-bound book of John Donne's poems, and he said, 'You weren't hooked on him at first, but after I'd read you a few of my favourites you began to appreciate him.'

It was a beautiful book, with its tooled-leather cover and gilt-edged parchment leaves. Just looking and stroking it was a delight. Then there was a miniature of a Siamese that could have been Schula, perfume in a cut-glass bottle, silken underwear, a silver-backed hairbrush and comb.

They made up stories round them all, and it was like remembering, until she sat on the rug, gifts piled around, brushing her hair now with the silver brush, coming up to her last birthday, never having been so pampered in her life.

He said, 'I nearly bought you a ring. After all, we'd known each other a long time. We knew we were good together. I knew I loved you.' Her heart leapt when he said that, and he went on, 'But I decided to wait till your next birthday before I asked you to marry me, and I brought you this.'

Marry him? It made Livvy stop brushing her hair and straighten up, blinking at him and at the painting he produced like a conjuror from behind a chair.

He propped it on the chair facing her, as if it was the climax of the game they were playing. 'How about that, then? A genuine Laurence Charles.'

She was suddenly chilled to the bone, as if she had been dragged from this warm room and thrust out into a winter's night. She stared at the picture, unable to speak, and at last he said, 'It's not that good. Not bad, but it's no Van Gogh.'

It hypnotised her, she couldn't look away. The colours were so bright, it looked new. A seascape with sunlight glinting gold on the sand and silver on the sea and a tall ship, sails billowing.

'Where did you get it?' she whispered.

'I've had friends scouting for me. One came up. It belonged to somebody who lived in the commune when Charles was here.'

The tip of her tongue licked her dry lips. 'Are they still alive?'

'Unfortunately, no. We're dealing with the son. While he was young the old man went through a spell of wanting to be an artist, but he ended up back home in the family business. Wholesale fruiterers and still doing nicely, so perhaps he made the right choice. And this isn't all.'

He thought she was thrilled with the discovery they were sharing. 'Letters. A bundle of them that he wrote to his girlfriend, a diary with sketches in the margin. They married when he went back, and she'd kept all his letters. I haven't read them yet. We'll go through them together tomorrow.'

It was a time-warp. The painting that looked new and the voice from the past. Someone who kept a diary must have named names, and if just once he mentioned Maybelle Murrin that would be enough to alert Corbin.

She asked, 'Where are the letters?'

'In the office.' She had to get to them first. Even if any of them were dangerous she could not risk destroying them, but she would be forewarned. So would Maybelle. Maybelle was in her eighties, for goodness' sake. All she needed to do was to shake her head and say, 'I don't remember.' But Livvy had to know what was in the letters.

Corbin said, 'It's late, you're tired.'

The strain must be showing, and in every way but one he could read her like a book. She said brightly, 'It's been a very exciting evening. What with this and that, and these.' She looked down at the gifts; they had been such magic, until the last one that meant the make-believe was over.

'Give Daisy the ones you've grown out of.'

The toys, the childish things. Livvy said, 'She'll think Christmas has come early, although Christmas could be here before Henry thinks Daisy deserves prezzies,' and he laughed and packed them back into the bag and helped her carry them upstairs.

All but the painting. That was taken into the office, and she watched as Corbin put it on the desk beside the yellowing envelopes tied with faded blue ribbon.

When everyone was asleep she would come down and fetch them and read them in her room. Tomorrow she would have to go through them again with Corbin, and she hoped desperately that there would not be a point when she would have to act astonishment, as if she could not believe she was seeing Maybelle's name.

In her bedroom he put down the bag, and she put the gifts she was carrying on the dressing-table and asked, 'What did I give you over the years, while you were giving me all these?'

He held her for a moment, looking down into her pale face. 'More than anyone else ever did,' he said. He kissed her gently and said, 'Goodnight,' and went quietly, closing the door behind him.

Livvy had to let at least an hour go by before she could risk creeping down, so she got ready for bed and lay there trying to relax. But she hadn't a hope, her mind was hyperactive. She'd known something like this was bound to happen sooner or later, and it was a lucky break that Corbin had waited to read the diary with her. He could have come back and sprung it on her without warning. 'Why did Maybelle say she knew nothing about the artists? She was often down there. She knew Laurence Charles.'

She didn't switch on the lights. Her eyes were used to the dark, and enough light came through the windows to show the banisters and the staircase. She crept as Henry said Daisy had, like a mouse, and when a stair creaked she cursed herself. Only a little creak, but it sounded like a pistol shot in the silence and immediately Luke started barking.

She cursed him too, although he stopped almost at once, and she tiptoed down the rest of the stairs and across the hall. Curtains were drawn in the office and she made her way to the patio window, letting in enough light to see where the letters lay.

She had them in her hands when a light came on from the hall and she moved fast and instinctively, putting the letters down again, switching on a light and walking to the door in the hall.

She had known it would be Corbin. She said, 'I'm glad to see you remembered the robe.' He wore a short dressing-gown in dark blue towelling. Bare-legged and bare-footed, he seemed to make no sound at all crossing the hall. She said, 'Couldn't you sleep either, or do you always investigate when Luke barks?'

He said, 'I couldn't sleep and I thought it might be you. What are you doing down here?'

'Looking at the picture again.' She walked around and stood, arms folded, facing it. 'It's a real find. I've been lying there thinking about it. I came down for another look and to make myself a drink.'

'May I join you?'

'Where?'

He grinned. 'Given the choice, I'd say your bedroom or mine.' Livvy shook her head. 'But as I'm not, how about the parlour? We could stir up the fire.' He picked up the letters. 'And read these.'

There was no chance now of her reading the diary before he did. Even if she said, 'I think a bedroom might be more fun,' which of course she could not, it would only be a delaying tactic. Corbin had slipped off the ribbon and was taking the top letter out of its envelope. 'Let's get acquainted with the Laurence Charles set,' he said. 'We might meet the Dark Lady.'

CHAPTER SIX

IN THE PARLOUR the ashes were grey, and pink where the wood still smouldered. Livvy took another log from the big copper cauldron by the fireplace and set it squarely on the embers. It wasn't cold in here, but she was in nightwear and Corbin was probably only wearing a robe. And if that diary mentioned Maybelle her blood would turn to ice. Little flames crept up, and she watched them for a moment, wishing she could throw the bundle of letters on the fire.

He was sitting on the chesterfield, reading the first page. 'They're in order,' he told her. 'He arrived here in May—Wallace Witts, aged twenty-one.'

He reached a hand to pull her down beside him. 'May till early November,' he said. 'Pity he didn't stick it out another month, but this is the year we want.'

The year he wanted. Just looking at the date made Livvy feel queasy, but she could understand why the future Mrs Witts had kept the letters, if it was only for the little sketches that went with them. He had left the commune, and gone back to marry his girl and spend the rest of his life selling fruit, but when he had started to keep this diary Wallace had been an artist.

Some of the sketches were scenes. He was living in the old farmhouse, and he had drawn that for her, describing the place and some of the people who were here. He drew them too, and Livvy could have snatched the letters from Corbin's hands, although as they were out of the envelopes he held them so that she could read as easily as he could, and with each page her eyes skimmed ahead looking for 'Maybelle'.

'Laurence Charles.' Corbin pounced on that. Laurence had an exhibition coming up. Laurence had a cottage. Wallace sketched neither, and by now he was missing his girl and the comforts of home.

He was at that garden party. 'The death-watch beetle's in the church timbers and it's a shilling a head to mix with the local nobs. They think we're rogues and vagabonds, but we'll be going, because the grub should be worth the money.'

'I like it,' said Corbin, and Livvy reached across him for the next letter. The food, it seemed, had been up to expectations, and there was no mention of Maybelle. 'I wonder if he was on the photograph,' Corbin mused. 'We must ask, his son might know.'

There were twenty-five letters in all, and until Corbin put down the last one she breathed shallowly, rigid with tension. It was only when she knew there was nothing in here to link Maybelle with Laurence that her eyes started smarting. She had hardly dared blink before as she devoured every page, and now they were stinging, making the room swim.

She put a hand in front of her face and Corbin put an arm around her shoulders, drawing her close. He began stroking her hair, and as she nestled against him his skin was warm and naked beneath his robe.

She might as well have been naked herself, for all the protection this flimsy covering was. Her hands had been reaching of their own volition to lock behind his head or to grip his shoulders and draw him closer still. But now her fingers stiffened and she put her hands flat on his chest, making a barrier between them.

She slid out of his embrace, her eyes dark and tortured, and he said, 'Why don't you let me love you?

What are you afraid of? You can't be scared of me. You know I'd rather hurt myself than hurt you. Hurting you would be hurting myself.'

Words wouldn't come. She sat there dry-eyed but sobbing inside, and Corbin went on, 'It can't be Andrew, but was there someone?'

'Why do you ask that?' she managed to ask.

'Because there's hurt. Or fear. Something that makes you wary.'

It was fear of herself. She wanted to stop fighting. She had never known what desire was before, blurring the mind as sensation took over. She had never been empty before, like someone starved and silently screaming with the pain of hunger. Once he really touched her she would cling to him as if he was life itself. But somehow she found the strength to hold back when he put his hands over the hands she was pushing against him and tried to draw them away.

He could have done, of course. He could have lifted her arms wide and left her open and defenceless, but she sobbed, *'No,'* and he asked again, 'Why?'

She must not struggle. She had been guilty of enough provocation already, asking for more control of him than any woman could expect. If it hadn't been for the diary she would never have come down here like this. The danger of what that might reveal had blinded her to a greater danger. She had already gone too far with Corbin, and if she got herself seduced she couldn't call it rape. She had to start talking and thank her stars he was still talking, not taking.

She stammered, 'Maybe it's Andrew. He thinks he and I—I've let him think——' That was true, but Andrew had no part in this and Corbin knew it. 'No,' he said.

'And Sonia. She's a warning. A man walked out on her two years ago and she's still reeling from the shock.'

'What has that got to do with us?' Nothing. She was making wild excuses so that he would let her go. Anything but the truth.

She said, 'It made me cautious, wary.' His grip on her wrists had loosened, and as he sat back she let her hands fall. She tried to joke, 'Cats are wary creatures,' but her lips wouldn't smile. The clockwork dog was still lying by the wall, overlooked when they collected the gifts, and Livvy tried again, desperately playing the make-believe, 'I know we've known each other for years, but you did say you were going to wait until my next birthday. We've been just good friends a long time, please don't rush me now.'

He said, 'I should be moving on.'

'What?'

'I could move into the cottage.'

'Laurence's? That wouldn't be very comfortable.' She said that as she thought it, and it sounded as if she didn't want him to go.

He said drily, 'It isn't very comfortable here at night, under the same roof as you, wanting you so badly.'

She was panicked again into pleading, *'Please,'* as she scrambled to her feet.

Then he smiled wryly, perhaps at her or perhaps at himself, and said, 'It's all right. Go to bed now. I'll get these back in order.'

She was still stammering, 'I'm sorry,' at the doorway, and she got one of his wicked grins.

'I might have done better if I hadn't put the robe on.'

She did grin at that. 'Boasting again,' she said, and ran upstairs to her room. She shot the bolt on the door, a thing she rarely did, although she knew that Corbin would not come. Perhaps she was scared of sleep-walking, because these nights her dreams were filled with longings.

What had nearly happened down there was the narrowest escape of her life. He could have made it happen so easily if he had stopped her talking. Words were all the defence she had when every inch of her was calling out for him.

If they made love it would have been wonderful, but in the morning nothing would have changed. She would still be cheating him because of another man who had died over half a century before she was born.

It had been best the way it was, nothing happening, even if she was going to cry herself to sleep now...

Next morning a subdued Daisy arrived in the kitchen. Sonia held her hand and they were a little later than usual. Corbin, Henry and Livvy were drinking a first cup of coffee, and Daisy's eyes swivelled towards Henry, who glared back. 'She's very sorry for causing all that trouble,' Sonia apologised for her. 'She came down for a glass of milk, and when she opened the kitchen door the dog got out.'

Daisy went on nodding, and Livvy thought, a likely tale.

'Hmm,' said Henry, but the night's rest had calmed him down and Daisy certainly looked contrite. 'We'll leave it at that, then.' He added, 'This time,' which meant that if there was a next time she would not get off so easily.

'And she'll say sorry to Aunt Maysie.' Sonia remembered that Maybelle had needed brandy after the fracas. 'She is all right this morning, isn't she?'

'She was last night,' said Livvy. 'Not pleased with Daisy, but she settled down. I'm going to take her a cup of tea up. Daisy can come too.'

She went into Maybelle's apartment first, leaving Daisy on the landing and gently rousing Maybelle from sleep.

As Maybelle sipped her tea, Daisy was ushered to the side of her bed and said in a very small voice, 'I'm sorry.'

'Came down for a glass of milk, I hear,' said Maybelle. Daisy shuffled her feet. 'Then it was an accident,' said Maybelle, 'and accidents can't be helped. But if I thought you let the dog out, being naughty, then I should be very cross indeed. You do understand that?' A nod, and Daisy backed away from the bed. 'Off you go,' said Maybelle, and Daisy went as fast as her legs could carry her.

Livvy smiled. 'Do you think she's learned a lesson?'

'If she has,' said Maybelle drily, 'it could be that grown-ups are gullible. How's Henry? I didn't like the colour of him last night.'

Livvy said, 'He's a better colour this morning. He's put her on probation. One more trick and he's clapping her in irons.'

Daisy was still in the hall when she got downstairs, standing outside the parlour door. It was open, Daisy had looked in and seen the toy dog, and she held it now, asking Livvy, 'Whose is this?'

'Mine,' said Livvy, then she relented. 'Bring it along.'

In the kitchen Daisy put it on the table and turned pleadingly to Livvy. Livvy said, 'I don't know about this. I think Henry should say whether Daisy can keep it.' Daisy switched to Henry. 'Corbin brought it back,' said Livvy. 'He brought a lot of things back.' She had to smile at Corbin then. 'And some were toys. Daisy just found this one, so what does Henry say?'

Henry thought about it while Daisy looked longingly at the toy, not daring to touch. When he said gruffly, 'All right,' she picked it up and scurried to a chair in the corner, keeping out of everyone's way in case he changed his mind.

Then, because it was the natural thing to say if Livvy was as excited about the find as Corbin believed she was,

Livvy asked, 'Can I tell them about the painting and the letters?'

He said, 'Of course,' and she went on, 'We've got a Laurence Charles painting and the diary of one of the artists who lived here at the time.' She was making it sound like a team effort, and that was how they both felt, because this was their story, happening on their doorstep.

They couldn't wait to read the diary and see the picture. They hurried into the parlour when Corbin told them where it was, and stared at the painting as if it were priceless. Sonia peered at the monogram 'LC', and Henry said, 'Laurence Charles—it's the real thing, isn't it? It's in tip-top condition.'

'It's been cleaned,' Corbin explained. 'The dealer who found it for me removed the grime.'

'Could have been painted yesterday,' said Henry. 'May we show Maybelle?'

There was no stopping them. When Livvy went upstairs with the breakfast tray, so did Henry with the painting.

Maybelle was at her usual little table, and Livvy said, 'Corbin's found a Laurence Charles painting,' trying to shield her for that moment, standing between her and Henry.

Maybelle looked blank. To Livvy it was like shutters coming down, but to Henry it simply meant that she had not quite heard. He repeated, 'A painting by Laurence Charles. The artist feller from Blackrock Chine.'

'Of course.' She blinked at the painting. 'Very nice.'

'And he's got a diary,' said Henry, 'that one of them kept that year.'

'I read it last night,' said Livvy quickly. 'It only mentioned Laurence once, about an exhibition he was planning. The man who kept the diary left in October.'

'Could have been painted yesterday,' said Henry. 'I knew you'd like to see it.' He placed it on a chair. 'Shall we leave it with you?'

'I think you should take it back to Corbin,' said Maybelle. 'It's his painting. And how are you feeling this morning, after last night?' Livvy took the picture away and left them talking about Daisy.

Maybelle was not cracking up, but that painting must have shocked her, and during the morning Livvy ran up to her apartment often, finding excuses, to reassure herself that all was well. It seemed to be. Maybelle was bright and chirpy every time Livvy looked in, and she ate her lunch and afterwards settled down for her afternoon nap.

Corbin had taken the letters to get them photostatted, and Livvy had worked hard, slapping on paint, and gone quietly upstairs again to make sure Maybelle was all right.

The door was locked, and Livvy knocked and rattled the knob, and when Maybelle opened it very slightly she almost pushed her way in, demanding, 'What did you do that for? Are you all right?'

'I might be if I was allowed some privacy.' Maybelle leaned on her walking stick and glared. She had been burning papers in the little fireplace that was never used. Radiators and an electric fire provided the heating in here, but now there were flames in the grate and Maybelle had been feeding them.

The cedar chest was open, with cards and papers scattered around. She must have perched awkwardly on the low chair by the fireplace, and she should never be handling fire. Livvy said, 'That chimney could catch, it hasn't been swept for years. And if anything fell on the carpet or on you, what would you do then with the door locked?'

On cue a blackened scrap of paper floated out, settling gently on the carpet. They both watched, but it didn't burn. Maybelle said, 'Corbin asked if I had any old photographs, so I thought I'd see if I had. There's a lot of rubbish in there. I'm clearing it out.'

She was not looking for photographs to give Corbin. She was out to destroy what could be her only link with Laurence Charles. The chest was empty, she had reached the bottom, and that could not have been easy for her, disabled as she was. Livvy wondered if she had opened the envelope and looked for the last time on the lovers that were Maybelle and Laurie, before she had put them into the fire.

By the fireplace there was another small heap of papers, photographs, envelopes, and the lilac envelope set aside from the piles. She had not burned it yet. It was the only one that mattered, and she must have sat there, making a funeral pyre of the rest until she found the courage to put this into the flames.

'It you're set on a bonfire, I'll do it for you.' Livvy went down on her knees before the fire.

Maybelle lowered herself on to the chair, sitting awry and wincing with pain, then pushed the pile closer with her stick covering the envelope, and saying sharply, 'Hurry up, then. The smoke's getting on my chest.'

'I could burn them downstairs.'

'I want it done here. I'm a sentimental old fool and I'm saying my goodbyes.' Maybelle smiled, quite gaily, then winced again. 'Old bones,' she said. 'Burn them for me, there's a good girl.'

Livvy fed the flames and there was smoke, and when she picked up the lilac envelope Maybelle coughed and turned her head away. Livvy put the rest on as quickly as she dared, and kept them in the fire basket with the walking stick. Sparks flew up as the paper flared, and when everything was black dust she looked at Maybelle.

The light that kept her young seemed to have gone out, and Livvy sprang up to take her in her arms. Maybelle whispered, 'I'm all right. I'm tired. I've missed my rest. I'll rest now.'

Livvy got her into bed, insisting she took a couple of her panic pills, then she went straight to the phone to ask the doctor to call.

She caught him at home and he came before evening surgery, waking Maybelle. 'Hello,' said Maybelle, 'what are you doing here?'

'I sent for him,' Livvy explained. 'You seemed very tired.'

'You call the doctor and wake me for that? Tell her, Clifford, old women get tired,' and Clifford Aslett smiled with her. He checked pulse and heart and chatted for a while, and when he came downstairs with Livvy an anxious Sonia and Henry were waiting for them. His report was fairly reassuring. Maybelle's heartbeats were irregular as ever, but her spirits were high. 'Just carry on looking after her,' he patted Livvy's arm. 'I know how well you do that.'

But today's ordeal would take its toll, and Livvy was scared. Corbin came back shortly after the doctor had left, calling Livvy's name as he came into the house and asking as she reached him, 'What's happened?'

She had thought she looked cheerful, but he sounded concerned, and she had to explain, 'I didn't think Aunt Maysie looked so good, but the doctor says there's no need to panic.'

'No need at all,' said Henry firmly. 'Got into a bit of a flap, eh, Livvy?'

'You're joking.' Corbin smiled. 'Livvy doesn't flap. She's a cool customer, aren't you, my pretty?'

She smiled too as he put an arm around her. 'So you say.' But she was doing things that were not cool. Not just with Corbin, although that relationship must go no further, but when she had slipped the lilac envelope into her hip pocket.

She could not destroy it, it would have been like sacrilege. It was hidden in her dressing-table drawer now, and even if Maybelle had not turned away Livvy could not have burned Laurie's love letter to her.

She had to be cool and careful, and it wasn't easy, although the next few days were not too hard.

In the mornings Corbin worked, finishing the Madeleine Smith script, and Livvy got on with her own tasks. Afternoons he planned and plotted around the data he had on Laurence, while she typed and generally assisted. Sometimes they went walking with Luke, and evenings they stayed home.

That week Livvy had no trouble with Corbin that was outside her own skin. Inside she was aching for him, but from the night he had tried to make love to her and she had held him off he seemed to be waiting for her to make the next move. She knew he thought she would come to him in the end, as though the game they played of knowing each other for years and having all the time in the world was true.

That week they were like loving friends and, when the curtains were drawn and the house was warm and shuttered for the night, it was good to have Corbin here. Sonia was brighter around him, she had hardly sighed since he'd come, and Henry called him, 'My boy,' like a long-lost son.

He didn't question Maybelle about Laurence Charles any more; he probably thought she had told him all she knew, and Maybelle flirted with him and enjoyed his company. Daisy was behaving so well that, if Livvy had not known she was thinking about those toys that Corbin had brought, she would have wondered if she was sickening for something.

On Friday night Daisy sat beside Corbin in the parlour, dressed in her warm red nightie, lapping up her bedtime story. Following the little sketches in the diary, which they had all seen, he had begun illustrating the stories he was spinning.

He had a talent for it. He had produced a Daisy that anyone could recognise, and her toys and the fantasy creatures they were meeting. Last night he had introduced her mother, glamorising a blushing Sonia; and there was Henry sailing the seven seas as a pirate with skull and crossbones flying. Tonight was Livvy's turn. She was the queen of a castle full of Siamese cats, and Daisy was squealing with delight, watching the moving pencil.

When he paused, she asked, 'Is it hard, drawing Livvy?'

'Very hard,' he said, and she wriggled off the sofa.

'I know where there's a picture of Livvy.'

'That would be useful.'

As they went out of the room, Sonia chuckled. 'I wonder what she's going to show him.'

Livvy went on with what she was doing, repairing a velvet frame that was peeling. 'We'll know soon enough. The worst of the lot, probably.' There were plenty of snaps around and Maybelle had a studio photograph. 'Depends where she's been rooting.'

She had squeezed in the glue and now she pressed it down, and suddenly her own words seemed to echo back at her. Daisy did root—she poked around, she found things.

The thought hit Livvy like a fist in the face, making her stagger as she jumped up and ran out into the hall.

There was no sign of them, and she shouted 'Daisy!' and went up the stairs two at a time. Her bedroom door was wide and the lights were on. Inside the room her dressing-table drawer was open and Corbin held the postcard. Without looking at Livvy he said, 'Go downstairs, Daisy.'

Daisy didn't argue. She dived through the doorway past a frozen Livvy, and Livvy heard a voice that had to be her own saying, 'Now you'll want to know why.'

'Don't bother, I'm working it out.' He sounded as if she had offered to help with a crossword puzzle. He went to the bedside lamp and switched it on, his back to her. 'So this was how he looked.'

Livvy sidled into the room. His shoulders were broad, he seemed to block out the light from the lamp, and although the room was brightly lit now it seemed to Livvy to be in shadow. 'He was a womaniser,' he said, 'and Maybelle was one of them. No big deal, surely, after all this time. So why were you both so desperate to hide it?'

He thought they were together in a conspiracy of silence, and she muttered miserably, 'She doesn't know I've got this, we've never talked about it.'

Someone was coming at a fast trot, and Sonia appeared in the doorway, looking flushed. 'She's been going through your things again, has she? She must have been after those toys—oh, I *am* sorry!'

Corbin said, 'Tell her the story's postponed for the night.'

'Oh, I *will*.' Sonia turned to Livvy, whose stony face probably looked resentful, and made a helpless gesture. 'It *was* naughty of her. She won't do it again, I *promise*.'

He shut the door as Sonia turned away, and a few moments later shot the bolt, and Livvy knew how a guilty prisoner must feel facing the gaoler. 'That sums it up,' he said. 'End of fairy-tale. Now, let's recap and have the truth. When did you find this?'

'Years ago.' As soon as she spoke she knew that she should have said, 'Last week,' but she felt brainwashed with all the strength drained out of her.

'So you've known all along that Maybelle and Laurence were lovers?'

She ventured, 'Things were different in those days. They might not have been what we call lovers.'

'And you are an expert on non-consummation.' There was a savage mockery in his voice. 'Were they having what we should call an affair?' There was the evidence of the sketch, and Maybelle's raving in her fever had told Livvy that this had been a passion that had swept away all control. She didn't speak, but after a moment she nodded, and he said softly, 'And how would you know that for sure unless you were told?'

'She told me nothing. I found this among some old papers in her room, and she's old and sick and I don't want her cross-questioned about it.'

'Who else knows? Henry? Sonia? Andrew?'

'No.'

'Nobody? You discussed it with nobody?'

'No.'

'Then you were hiding more than a sixty-years-old love-affair.' Corbin spoke deliberately and slowly, and she was trapped. He would destroy them all, and she hated him for it. Even if she refused to say another word he would get there now, answering his own questions and never taking his eyes off her. She was cornered. He was watching her like a hawk and she felt his talons in her heart.

He was summing it up, getting closer all the time. 'No one linked her name with Laurence Charles. There were interviews galore about him in the press, but Maybelle's

name never came up. Their affair was kept well under
wraps. She didn't want it known then, and that's under-
standable if she was engaged to Edward Cramer, but it
can't matter now. She might prefer not to talk about it,
but you'd have had it in proportion. From this distance
you wouldn't even be shocked, so why are you scared
witless?'

The blood had been draining from her cheeks as he
was speaking; she must be chalk-white by now. 'What
else have you found out? When *did* she leave here?'

Through stiff lips she whispered, 'I don't know.'

'You do,' he said softly, 'and I will.' With his re-
sources he could find out when Maybelle had sailed for
America. She had said she'd been long gone when
Laurence had died, but she hadn't been, and Livvy
wanted to claw his implacable face.

She gasped, 'You might get yourself a story, but it
isn't going to look good if you harass an old woman
into her grave. Don't you have any ethics, any conscience? Of course, it wouldn't matter to you that I'd
hate you for it until I died.'

'Which you will,' he said. He put the postcard into
his pocket, and she wondered wildly if there was any
way of getting it back. He was near enough, but she
could never again slip her arms around him. She could
not take it and he would never return it.

He reached for her. His grip on her shoulders was a
bruising pressure that she would have shrunk from if she
could, but he held her upright and close like a rag doll.
'It's hate I'm looking at now,' he said, and smiled into
her frightened face. 'You're not acting now, are you, my
pretty? This is the real thing, straight from the heart.'

She felt her heart lurch with terror. She had never
before looked into the eyes of anyone and been afraid
of the devil she saw there. He was incredibly strong, he

was hurting her, and this was not all he could do. There was a red flame in his eyes, although his voice was gentle as a lover's.

'I've been a pushover. You conned me from that first five minutes. You knew everything I was learning about this case as soon as I did, and if I'd come across that sketch anywhere but in your room I might have believed you hadn't known. You had me right *there*.'

He loosed her shoulders, grabbed one of her hands and placed it in his, closing her fingers hard with the other hand. Livvy stared down. He meant she'd had him in the palm of her hand, and so she had, but no more. She looked up at him, agonised, and he said, 'You could have done it. I'd have left the old woman alone if the going got rough, for your sake. For your sake.' He grinned at that. 'You don't look much now, but it's a shame you've stopped cheating. When I wanted to know what happened that night, where was Maybelle when the lights went out for Laurence, how would you have stopped me asking? Like this?'

He pulled her to him, an arm around her, a hand behind her head, and kissed her. She gagged when he let her head loll back, and he snapped, 'Don't act the lily with me! You put everything you've got on offer. Every hold-off was a come-on. I could have had you any time if I hadn't been a bloody fool.'

She was not submitting, but it made no odds. Corbin could force her apart, find her, take her, and she moaned, 'This is obscene!' Then she was flung across the bed against the wall to lie there in a huddled heap.

He said, 'I'll collect my stuff tomorrow. You wouldn't be safe with me in the house tonight. Not because I want to get into your bed, but because I'd get more satisfaction from beating the hell out of you.'

The controlled force had her cringing. She wished he would hit her. He seemed more menacing holding back his anger. 'You cheating little bitch,' he said softly. He walked out of the room, and minutes later Livvy heard his car being driven away.

She had to get off the bed and get to the bathroom, turn on the shower and try to wash herself clean. It wasn't what he had done to her that she needed to wash away, so much as the way he had looked at her.

She should never have tried to con him. She should not have let him believe she was falling in love, leading him on, seeming to promise. 'You wouldn't believe how many cheats and liars there are in the world,' he had said, and now he knew that right from the beginning she had been double-crossing him. As a journalist and as a man she had played him for a fool. And in the end all she had achieved was to make him her bitter enemy.

The Laurence Charles story would hit the headlines now, even if she managed to keep Corbin away from Maybelle. Dr Aslett might back her up, if she told him why, and then she would stand guard and not answer the door or the phone. But Corbin had the sketch; he would find out that Maybelle had been here when Laurence had died, and the house and Maybelle would be under siege.

Her head was throbbing and pounding, and she ached when she moved. She sat on the bed, hands clasped over her head, head sunk on her chest, wishing she could crawl away and die.

'Where's Corbin gone?' asked Sonia; then a good look at Livvy stopped her dead. 'Oh, heavens!' Her lips framed the words with no sound coming out, and then in a strangled cry, 'What did he *do* to you?'

That brought Livvy out of shock and nearly into hysteria. She sat up and got off the bed. Her clothes were dishevelled and her hair was wild. She took off the shirt and pulled on a sweater and sat down on a stool in front of the dressing-table. She reached for the silver-backed brush Corbin had given her, but shuddered as she touched it, and left it lying there, smoothing down her hair with both hands.

Her shoulders were shaking, and a horrible laughter was rising up in her. What had Corbin done to her? Much the same as she had done to him. Gone for the kill, where her pride was concerned. She looked dreadful and felt dreadful, and he would be driving that car in the kind of rage that could take him over the cliff. If it did, there was the problem solved.

She heard herself whimper and shook her head at her reflection in the mirror, because he was in control of himself and he would be in control of the car. He would get where he was going safely and she was in big trouble here, but she wanted him to be safe. The hysteria in her subsided and she turned to face Sonia.

Daisy wasn't here, and Livvy was glad of that, but Sonia had been struck dumb after her shriek. She waited now in hushed horror, her hands clasped as if she was praying.

Livvy said, 'We had a—disagreement,' and nearly giggled, which would have been hysteria, but she could not explain to Sonia. Right now she wanted to be alone, to get herself together and decide what she would tell and who she would tell it to. She said, 'I'm all right.'

'You don't look all right.' Sonia had found her voice and Livvy was far from all right—anybody could see that. Corbin had driven off into the night and Livvy was looking as though she had been in a rough-house.

'I wasn't raped,' Livvy said bluntly.

'Of *course* not,' responded Sonia, although she was wondering.

'But there was a sort of a struggle,' said Livvy.

'But he didn't?'

'No.'

'Well, I suppose that's all right, then,' said Sonia. 'I suppose you know what you want.' She was still disapproving. 'Or what you don't want. Although you could have fooled me. I thought you two were sleeping together.'

Half an hour or so later Livvy followed her downstairs. By now Livvy looked composed, pale but no longer shaking, although how she felt inside was a different matter. Sonia was waiting for her. Daisy had been sent to bed and in the parlour Henry and Sonia had the television on. Neither was watching the screen, and when Livvy walked into the room Sonia got up and turned off the set.

Henry cleared his throat and said, 'Hrrm—well, I've got something to see to. I'll see you later.'

He was embarrassed, and Livvy watched him heading for the staircase, leaving them alone, and knew that whatever Sonia had been telling him was nothing to what he was soon going to learn.

Sonia asked, 'Corbin is coming back, isn't he?'

'Some time, to collect his things.'

'Then I want to talk to you.' Sonia waited until Livvy sat down before she went on. 'You can always tell me to mind my own business, but we are friends, and you've always been very good to me, and I just don't understand why you're treating Corbin like this.'

A wan smile twisted Livvy's lips. 'Now you think I should be sleeping with him? You were warning me against that a few days ago. I thought you fancied him yourself.' It was easier to let Sonia have her say. Refuse to listen to her and she could be following Livvy around, and when Livvy talked to Henry it had to be in utter privacy.

'Of *course* I fancy him,' said Sonia, practically wringing her hands in her eagerness to stress her point of view, 'but I never thought he'd look at me. Of course I like him, but I knew I'd never *get* him in a million years. But you two this week! Well, he hasn't been able to keep his hands off you, and you've been all over him.'

Livvy said, 'I have not.' It had been a time of companionship, but it was a phoney closeness and it was over.

'Of course you have!' Sonia shrilled. 'And when Andrew rang you, you wouldn't go out.'

Andrew had phoned a couple of times and Livvy's excuses had seemed sound to her. She had been busy. 'If Corbin went further than you were ready for,' said Sonia firmly, 'it's your fault. You gave him all the signals and I don't think you ought to blame him. I think you ought to ask him to come back again.'

'Just like that?'

'You could. He's crazy about you.'

Crazy could be the word. Livvy could still feel his grip on her, and it was nothing like the thrill that his touch had once sent tingling through all her nervous system. It had been punishing, meant to hurt. When Corbin came back it would be a grim meeting, not a tender reunion, and Livvy could not sit here any longer humouring Sonia, who had no idea at all what had happened and what was going to happen.

The sketches were still on the sofa, with Livvy as queen of the Siamese cats on a clipboard, and Livvy said, 'We can put those away; he won't be telling any more bedtime stories.'

'I bet he will,' said Sonia. 'You're never going to let a man like him get away.'

She still couldn't understand why Livvy should have turned so prudish when those last few days anybody could see they were mad about each other. Sonia wanted her friend to be happy, and Corbin was the right one for Livvy, not Andrew. But that would leave Andrew out in the cold, and Andrew was a nice man. She had always known somebody like Corbin Radbrook was way out of her league, but if Livvy turned Andrew down then there was just an outside chance that he might notice Sonia.

Henry was in his room. He had a book in his hands and a glass on the table beside him, and he had heard Livvy coming. Sonia had come downstairs and hustled Daisy off to bed, and then informed Henry that Livvy and Corbin had had a row and that was why Corbin left. A lovers' quarrel, and Livvy was upset and angry. Sonia was going to talk to her because Sonia thought that she was being stupid.

Henry, who thought Livvy's IQ was probably double Sonia's, felt she should leave well alone and had got himself out of the way. When he heard Livvy's footsteps he didn't know whether she would be annoyed or amused. But he hoped they would have a laugh together at Sonia setting herself up as an agony aunt, and Livvy would reassure him that the tiff was much ado about nothing.

One look at her face told him this was no laughing matter. It got him to his feet so fast that he dropped his book as he hurried towards her, urging her, 'Come and sit down, m'dear, it can't be that bad.'

Livvy sat. Henry had closed the door and now he was pouring her a whisky, and she said, 'I'll take it neat.'

He had never known her do that, nor seen her gulp down the spirit and then sit back gasping and grimacing.

'You have no idea how bad,' she said. 'You'd better sit down.'

He slumped down again into his own seat, his eyes fixed on Livvy. 'Bless my soul,' he muttered.

'We can do with a blessing,' she said. 'I need your help. It's to do with what brought Corbin here. This script he's writing. When Maybelle was ill, when she broke her hip, one night she was delirious. I was the only one with her, so nobody else heard, but she was talking about Laurence Charles.'

Henry tried to butt in. 'Something she remembered from when she was a slip of a girl?'

'She was about my age, and they had a love-affair,' Livvy went on. 'She was reliving the end of it, when she was going out of her mind with jealousy. She went through it as if it were happening again, and it broke my heart.'

'Poor girl,' said Henry gruffly. He could have meant Livvy or Maybelle, his leathery old face was full of pity. 'But she was happy with Edward, so what does this matter now?'

Livvy said heavily, 'She sailed the day after Laurence died. She was here that last night. The quarrel could have been that last night.'

'Again, it might not,' said Henry.

'Corbin knows she lied. He's going to ask questions. He has a sketch that Laurence made of himself and Maybelle smiling at each other, and he might as well have drawn them in each other's arms, it's that plain. Then there are the names underneath, and she signed herself Maybelle Charles. She kept it all these years and nobody knew, and she tried to burn it last week. She thinks it is burned, but I hid it, and just now Corbin found it.'

She let all that sink in. The lines on Henry's face grew deeper still, and at last he said, 'That's what you quarrelled about?'

'Yes.'

'When he comes back,' said Henry, 'we'll have a little chat, the three of us, and ask him to leave Maybelle out of it. He's getting a nice enough story together without dragging her in.'

Henry did not believe that Maybelle was implicated in her lover's death, and he imagined that Corbin Radbrook would be as trusting. But Corbin more than suspected, he *knew*. The moment Daisy put that postcard into his hand, his reporter's instinct had taken over. Before then he had been so infatuated with Livvy that he hadn't been seeing straight.

The idea of a little chat influencing him now was pathetic. Henry couldn't see what was staring him in the face. Even if she told him, She said she killed Laurence—he would insist that Livvy had misheard.

She must warn Maybelle, and that would mean explaining how Corbin had got the sketch and how Livvy had known. But not that Maybelle had said in her fever, 'I killed Laurie.' And all Livvy could do now was pray that Maybelle would find the strength never to say it again.

'We won't mention this to her until we've seen Corbin,' said Henry. He meant until after the chat that was going to change nothing. But it was getting late, and Maybelle might as well have one more fairly peaceful night. Henry, too. He might lie awake, worrying a little, but there was no point in Livvy warning him now that, thanks to her, they had an enemy without mercy.

'Don't tell Sonia either,' he said. 'You haven't mentioned it to her, have you?' She shook her head and he

nodded approvingly. 'Good, good, it's no concern of
hers, and Maybelle wouldn't like it.'

But Sonia was going to know, everyone was going to
know. And Maybelle Murrin was going to be suspected,
maybe accused, of far worse than a secret love-affair.

Livvy said, 'We'll leave it till tomorrow.' As she passed
him she bent to kiss his cheek and said, 'Thank you,'
because she loved him and the bad times were coming,
and he smiled up at her.

'Don't worry your pretty head.'

She went up the staircase slowly to the top floor.
Corbin would never call her 'my pretty' again. 'You don't
look much now,' he had said, and she knew how she
must look to him. Ugly to the bone, and that was how
she felt.

The cats came to meet her as she moved across the
room. Aunt Maysie was in bed, rather earlier than usual,
and Livvy asked if there was anything she wanted. She
said no, and Livvy said, 'Goodnight, then,' and shut the
door on Schula, who would have followed her out.

Sonia was on the landing below, and as Livvy walked
down the stairs she said, 'I've been looking in Corbin's
room. He took most of his papers with him, but he hasn't
cleared his room. I can't find his shaving tackle, though,
nor his pyjamas, so perhaps he's only going to be away
overnight, because his clothes are still there.'

Sonia had been playing detective, and finding out how
little Corbin had left with had cheered her up.

'He doesn't wear pyjamas,' said Livvy.

'How do you know?'

Livvy shrugged and walked past Sonia towards her
own room. Sonia trotted close behind. 'Livvy, when he
does come back, you will make it up with him, won't
you? It can't have been that much of a disagreement
really.'

Livvy said wryly, 'Wars have started with less.'

'Don't talk so *stupid*!' Sonia exploded. 'The way you two look at each other shows how you feel about each other.'

Opening her bedroom door, Livvy said, 'It did that all right tonight. I looked at him and saw a man I'd run a mile from, and he looked at me and saw something he wouldn't even wipe his feet on.'

She left Sonia dumbstruck again in the corridor outside, and leaned against the door in the darkened bedroom overwhelmed by a terrible feeling of loneliness. As though the world was ending. And for all the hope she could see for the future, her world *was* ending.

CHAPTER SEVEN

NEXT morning, down in the kitchen, Sonia noted the dark shadows under Livvy's eyes and said, 'Somebody didn't get much sleep last night.' She didn't add, Missing Corbin? but her expression did, and Livvy, who had hardly slept at all, made no reply.

Livvy was the only one who didn't want to see Corbin again. He was going to destroy their cosy little world, and she was sorry for them. For Sonia, who was trying to matchmake two bitter enemies, and for Henry. As Livvy poured that first cup of tea to take upstairs, Henry whispered, 'Not a word to Maybelle.' He thought he was a knight in shining armour, but he didn't realise he was up against a man who was as deadly as a hand grenade.

When Livvy carried in the breakfast tray and Maybelle got her first real look at her, even Maybelle's old eyes could see that something was very wrong. She asked anxiously, 'What's the matter? Aren't you feeling well?'

'I had a row with Corbin last night.'

'Oh, *no*! Oh, Livvy, you and Corbin shouldn't be quarrelling. Now, what is it all about?'

Henry strolled in, and Livvy knew that he had not trusted her not to alarm Maybelle. As Livvy left them she heard Maybelle say plaintively, 'Livvy says she's quarrelled with Corbin.'

Henry chuckled. 'You know what the young ones are like. I'm sure it's nothing serious.'

Corbin might be returning for his luggage, but he had cleared files and equipment from the office. There was nothing of his left on the desk or in the drawers. The painting had gone, and the letters. There was no sign now that he had ever worked in here, with Livvy beside him and Luke stretched out on the rug.

Automatically she moved her own things back into the empty drawers and the empty spaces. A few early Christmas cards had started arriving, and she got out her personal address book and began signing cards and addressing envelopes. But she made slow work of it. Most of the time she just sat, staring at nothing, waiting.

She knew when Corbin came, because Sonia flung open the door and hissed, 'He's here, aren't you coming?'

Henry was going to bring him in here, anyway. There was no need for Livvy to go out and meet him, and she was not at all sure that her legs would carry her. No sleep and no food were making her feel faint—that and the sheer dread of facing him again. She shook her head, and Sonia said, 'You're so stubborn and so *stupid*!' and banged the door.

A few minutes passed. Livvy addressed another card in a jerky writing she hardly recognised. Corbin had come to collect his belongings, and he would be packing clothes into cases in the bedroom. But Henry would try to get him in here to see Livvy before he left, and she couldn't hide behind closed doors for ever.

She pressed on the arms of the chair, levering herself up, and that was when the door opened and Henry brought Corbin in, and she sagged back into her seat. She saw the cases in the hall just outside and she saw Henry, but at first she couldn't look straight at Corbin, although it was as though his shadow fell across her.

She could guess the words Henry had used: Can you spare a few minutes? Livvy and I would like to have a little chat with you. And she said, 'There's nothing to discuss, is there?'

Corbin said, 'Between us? No.'

But he looked enquiringly at Henry, who said, 'Livvy's been telling me, seems Maybelle was talking about this artist feller when she was delirious, after her fall, you know. Seems they were pretty close one time.'

'So it seems,' said Corbin, and Henry, with the air of one who is going to ask a small favour, dropped his voice to a confiding level.

'Maybelle's kept it to herself all these years. She's no idea now that Livvy knew, much less me, and it would embarrass her if it did become common knowledge— folk gossiping and that. She was only a girl at the time. I mean to say, does it have to come out? Best forgotten, eh?'

He was wasting his breath appealing to Corbin, and it would have been all the same if he had been offering a bribe worth a king's ransom.

Livvy knew that nothing was going to stop Corbin writing that last scene. He was unreachable and cynical, looking older again than his thirty-two years, and no one in this house was a friend any more. Poor old Henry could count on no favours, although now he was sounding as if he had come up with the perfect solution. 'Better still, is there any chance of you jacking in the whole idea?'

Even Corbin looked surprised at the cheek of that. 'You mean tearing up the script?'

Henry beamed. 'Bright feller like you—soon find something else to write about.'

'It isn't that simple. I'm committed to producing a script on this case. It's down in my contract.'

Livvy knew that he was playing cat and mouse, laughing at them. But Henry thought a smile was a good sign, and when Corbin said, 'But I'll write it as I see fit,' Henry seized his hand and shook it vigorously.

'Couldn't ask for more—leave it with you, then. And you know you'd be very welcome back.'

Livvy said sharply, 'Do let's stop wasting our time.'

'Thank you, but I was finding it distracting trying to work here.'

Henry took that to mean Luke and the cats and Livvy, and felt he understood. 'Of course,' he said. 'Where are you staying?'

'At the cottage,' said Corbin.

'But we will be seeing you?'

'Rely on it.' He looked briefly at Livvy, and she made herself stare back. He had had enough entertainment here without the satisfaction of seeing her cringe. As he picked up his cases, Henry signalled—follow him, say goodbye; and she came round the desk, sorely tempted to hit Henry over the head with something heavy.

In the doorway Sonia pounced on her. 'Is he going? He isn't, is he?'

Livvy had to get away from them before she screamed at them, and there was no escape in the house. The worst had happened and she had to stand up to Corbin with no back-up from anybody, but she was no longer scared. She had behaved badly, but so had he. What he had done last night was unforgivable. She would stroll over to where he was loading his luggage into his car and say, When Henry said you would be welcome back, he forgot that this is my house and in my house you are not welcome.

He heaved in the biggest case and turned to face her. She expected to hear Luke growling, but the great shaggy dog was quiet for once, and Corbin waited for her to speak.

He had left her last time sobbing on the bed, but she would never cower in front of him again. She said, 'I don't have to tell you, do I, that Henry's appeal was his own idea? He's a gent of the old school, is Henry, and he had this crazy idea that you're a gentleman too.'

'Not only a gentleman, but an idiot,' said Corbin. 'An easy mistake, from the way I've been carrying on.' He laughed, and if they were watching from the house it must have looked friendly. 'But you can tell him I'm neither.'

Instinctively Livvy looked at the strong fingers that had held her so cruelly, and he followed her gaze and raised his right hand. She tensed, although he was only opening the car door to get behind the wheel.

'Don't panic,' he said. He sat there, with the door still open. 'This morning I've no urge to slap you or lay you. You'd fall apart if I hit you, and sex with you I'd pay to avoid.'

He shut the door and started up the engine, and left her standing in the empty forecourt with an icy wind blowing. She almost ran after him, screeching, I wouldn't let you touch me to keep me out of gaol! But that would have shown what a state she was in, and although it was infuriating that he was getting away with such an offensive remark it was just as well that he had driven off.

She whirled around and strode back towards the house. She had to force some food down or she would be getting light-headed. Beside her, Sonia sounded as if she was repeating something she had asked before. 'Well, is it all right?'

Livvy said, 'Not very, no,' and marched on towards the kitchen.

She had the larder door open when Henry came bustling in, rubbing his hands. 'Well, m'dear, have we cracked it?'

She blinked at him, 'What?' but Henry's elation persisted.

'I think we managed that pretty well. I don't think he'll do anything to hurt Maybelle. Or you. He's got a very soft spot for you.' He beamed at her with twinkling eyes, and he had never been so wrong about anything.

She said wearily, 'Dear old Henry, he doesn't have a soft spot in his whole body. My first impression was the right one, and he can do more than hurt us. He's a hitman, a killer.'

Henry was deeply shocked. 'No! Oh, no!'

She mimicked bitterly, 'Yes. Oh, yes,' and an alarm bell rang in the kitchen that had only rung when they were testing it in the years since it had been installed.

Livvy ran. In the hall, the second downstairs bell was ringing, and Sonia was staring at it, asking, 'Is that Aunt Maysie?'

Of course it was Aunt Maysie. This was the panic alarm from her apartment. Livvy ran past Sonia and up the staircase with Henry puffing behind her. She nearly tripped over Mischa, who darted on to the top landing as she reached it, and as she hurtled into the room the ringing stopped.

Maybelle, sitting in her chair, had been pressing the button with the end of her walking stick. She had wanted somebody up here fast, but she didn't look ill, and Livvy gasped, 'Why did you ring?' Maybelle peered beyond her and Henry towards Sonia, who was just arriving in the doorway.

'That's all right, dear,' she said, dismissing Sonia, and as Henry shut the door on her Maybelle turned accusingly on Livvy. 'Corbin's gone again.' She must have been watching from her window. 'What are you thinking of letting him go? You and Corbin——'

'No,' said Livvy.

'And don't start on about Andrew!' Maybelle wailed. 'Because Andrew can't hold a candle to Corbin, and whatever you quarrelled about won't change that.'

She was distressing herself for the wrong reason, but the time had come to tell her what Corbin Radbrook could do. Livvy said, 'I'll have to tell you why we quarrelled—and please try to keep calm.'

'If you're going to tell me again that he's set on seducing you,' Maybelle rolled her eyes in exasperation, 'then you're acting like a silly schoolgirl, and I'm surprised at you.'

Livvy said, 'Forget the seducer. That isn't his style and it never was. It's the journalist we're having trouble with.'

'It's about this artist feller,' said Henry.

Maybelle was still waiting for Livvy to speak, and Livvy said, 'You talked about him when you were delirious. You don't remember that?'

'No.'

'No one else heard. Only me.'

'She told me only yesterday,' said Henry. 'Why didn't you tell us before?'

'It was so long ago.' Maybelle had leaned her stick by the chair, and the knuckles of her folded hands were white. 'Is this why you and Corbin quarrelled?'

Livvy said, 'I didn't burn the sketch,' and Maybelle flinched at that. 'Daisy found it. She thought it was a drawing of me and she gave it to Corbin.'

'That child!' roared Henry, glad to have someone to blame and settling for Daisy, although neither Maybelle nor Livvy was listening to him.

Maybelle said, 'So Corbin thinks you've been—what do they call it, withholding evidence?'

'That's about it.'

'Does he know I was there?'

She must mean the night Laurence Charles died, and Livvy said, 'Yes.'

'Then I must talk to him. You fetch him. Do you know where to find him?'

'I think so.' Livvy took Maybelle's hand, her fingers lightly circling a wrist, checking for the pulse-rate, and the old woman, realising what she was about, held steady with a spark of mischief. 'Not so bad,' said Livvy. Nor was it. And now Maybelle was reassuring Livvy.

'It will be all right.'

'Of course it will,' said Livvy.

Sonia was waiting at the bottom of the staircase to ask, 'What was all that about?'

'She wants Corbin,' said Livvy.

'Don't we all?' said Sonia. 'So?'

'So I'm fetching him,' said Livvy, going into her bedroom and leaving Sonia wishing wistfully that she could fetch a man like Corbin any time she wanted.

But the last thing Livvy wanted to do was to bring Corbin back here to hurt them all. Sonia imagined that Livvy was glamorising herself and choosing her outfit to go and meet her lover, but for Livvy it was more like preparing to face her executioner.

It couldn't matter less what she looked like; she didn't give her face a second glance. She just went through her wardrobe for her warmest clothes, because it was going to be a bitterly cold climb up to the cottage.

She put on an Aran sweater and a pair of fashion ski-pants, topping them with a hooded jacket, and sheepskin mittens. Her oldest boots were her warmest, with knitted socks inside.

It got dark early this time of year, and already the leaden skies seemed to be heavier. The wind was keen, with the smell and the taste of snow, and for a moment she hesitated. Then she looked back at the house and saw the faces at the windows, and she knew if she refused to go they would all be badgering her again.

As she climbed into her car she said aloud, 'I'm so *tired*!' She had been fighting a battle ever since Corbin Radbrook had arrived here. Now she had lost all she was fighting for, and of course she felt weary and sick at heart.

Perhaps she wouldn't even try to reach the cottage. Just drive to a deserted promenade and watch the cold sea crashing in. Or visit friends. Andrew probably was the one she should be heading for, but ten minutes later she ended in the empty field, with the stile that led to the track over the downs.

Empty except for Corbin's car, so he had come straight here. Little flakes of snow were falling as she parked beside the station wagon, got out of her own car and walked around it. The cases had gone. He would have been heavily loaded climbing up with them, but he still had a good start on her.

She could leave a note stuck under his windscreen, if she had something to write it with. She poked around her glove compartment, but found nothing better than an old eyeliner. She tried to write 'Ring Sweet Orchard' on the back of an envelope, but the eyeliner crumbled and she changed her mind and put the envelope in her pocket.

If she moved she could be up there, deliver her message and down again, before the snow had time to settle. She must start as she would have to go on from now on, facing up to him. Leaving a note was a cop-out, and she walked briskly to the stile.

She wouldn't remember the last time, when Corbin had held out a hand for her to hold, and his touch had warmed her, although the wind had been cold.

But it was nothing to this wind. This wind was wicked, driving the snowflakes into her face, and she pulled up her hood and put down her head and began to jog up the winding path, forcing herself on until she was nearly out of breath. She stopped for a breather then, gasping and trying to turn her back on the wind. But this was worse than moving, you could freeze standing still, and she didn't have to stay on the winding track. She could take a shorter cut through the dead bracken and gorse, pacing herself sensibly. She must be out of condition, because she was finding it killingly hard-going.

Her boots felt like lead dragging on her feet through the undergrowth, and her thick coat seemed a dead weight. She would not have believed it was so far. With Corbin it had seemed no distance at all. Nor, long ago, when she had come alone. But now there was a time when her head began to spin and she began to wonder if she was going to make it. She checked that panicky fear at once. This was a hill, not a mountain, a snow flurry, not an avalanche, and she could see a light burning up there. She had to stop floundering and panting and plod steadily, keeping her eyes on the lamp in the window which was getting nearer with every step.

Watching the lamp did her a power of good. It had not been lit for her, but it was where she was going. And when she could make out the shape of the cottage, and she was close enough to have been within shouting distance if it hadn't been for the wind, she stood still and breathed slowly.

The icy air drawn deep into her lungs was like a knife stab, making her choke, and she was still coughing when she took off her mitten and rapped on the door.

Luke started to bark and almost at once the door was opened. Corbin recognised her, although the hood was still covering most of her face. She was feeling distinctly woozy, but she knew he recognised her from the way he said, 'What the hell do you want?'

Warm air was coming from the room. 'I want to come in.'

'No.'

Livvy explained quite patiently, 'I'm freezing out here.'

'Tough.'

'I have a message for you.'

'You've got nothing for me that's getting you through this door.'

The snow stuck to her, turning the blue coat and pants to a glittering grey. She blinked away the flakes that were tangled in her eyelashes and making everything swim around her. Then, with no more than a faint feeling of surprise, she was swimming herself, slipping down into darkness...

She opened her eyes and saw Luke and, without moving her head, the sofa she was lying on and the room she was in. From just behind her Corbin said, 'Don't ask "Where am I?" or I'll murder you.'

She knew where she was all right and what had happened, and it was odd, because she had never fainted before in her life. She said, 'Better not. People know I'm here.'

It had left her feeling slightly sick, and for now she kept still. He said, 'That was a smart move. I noticed when you *fainted*,' he put a doubting emphasis on the word, 'you fell in, not out.'

She said incredulously, 'If I'd fallen outside you'd have shut the door and left me lying there?'

'Right.'

He might have done that. She sat up to get a better look at him, as if she couldn't credit what she was hearing. 'You don't believe I did faint.' She had eaten nothing for nearly twenty-four hours and she had hardly slept a wink last night, and then there was all the stress and climbing up here. She knew why she had blacked out. But none of this would get any sympathy from him.

'I wouldn't believe you,' he said, 'if you told me it was snowing.'

The shutters had not been closed. The lamp burned in one window. Against the other the snow was whirling, and Livvy had to get down through that and back to her car. She said, 'The message was from Maybelle. She knows you have the sketch and she wants to talk to you.'

'Have you rehearsed what she's going to say?'

'No.'

'Then it should be riveting. I'll be along tomorrow.'

'Fine,' she said. Corbin had moved into the kitchen section, and she edged herself off the sofa. She had made a speedy recovery. She could stand and walk, and it must have been a brief blackout because the heat of the room had not yet melted the snow from her clothes; patches still encrusted her. She picked up the mitten she must have dropped from the floor, put it on and said, 'Goodbye.'

Her nostrils twitched to a savoury smell. She was not hungry, but she *had* fainted, and if that had happened out there she could have been in a bad way before she came round or anyone found her. It might happen again going back. Water was dripping from her, and she asked, 'May I dry my coat?'

The Calor gas heater was giving out a real heat. Corbin said, 'Yes,' but, when she started to thank him, 'Don't push your luck, it's already run out.'

'Don't I know it!' she muttered ruefully. 'The first real snow of the winter and I'm here for it.'

He closed the shutters, blocking out the swirling snow, and she put her coat over the back of the chair, as near to the fire as she dared, where the steam rose from it. Then she pulled off her sodden boots, leaving herself in thick red knitted socks, and wishing she could add her ski-pants. They were damp too, and her sweater was long enough to pass as a mini-dress, but it would have been too awful if he had thought she was trying to look sexy.

That proved she was still not quite right in the head. He would know she would never try that trick again, and she wouldn't look sexy, anyway, just silly.

He fed Luke in the kitchenette as Livvy sat by the fire, and when he asked if she wanted some soup she said eagerly, 'Oh, please!' She explained, 'I missed lunch,'— and supper and breakfast, although she didn't mention that—and when Corbin brought over a steaming mug with a spoon in it she reached out gratefully.

It was a hearty vegetable brew and there was no need for him to warn her it was scalding hot, the heat warmed her fingers through the thick pottery. In any case he probably would not have told her, because he said nothing else to her. He completely ignored her, eating at the table himself and reading a book.

Livvy swallowed slowly, feeling stronger as she got the soup down, but even when she took the mug back and said, 'Thank you,' he nodded, without looking up from his book or speaking. She left the mug and spoon in the sink and padded over to the door.

The wind and snow whipped in and she hurriedly shut the door again. It would be easy to take a wrong turn out there, and she asked with exaggerated politeness, 'Would it inconvenience you if I stayed until I can see my hand in front of me?'

'It wouldn't inconvenience me if you fell off the cliff,' he said. 'If you are staying, just keep quiet.'

She didn't thank him this time. He was doing nothing for her. It was his fault she was stuck up here; why couldn't he have gone back to the motel? If his car hadn't been down there she wouldn't have risked climbing up, and they would be worrying about her at home when she didn't come back. But there was nothing she could do about that. And now he was typing, that damned typewriter clicking away, beating a hellish tattoo on her temples.

Her jacket was almost dry, so she got into it and sat on the sofa with the hood covering her ears and most of her face, ostentatiously shutting herself off from this room and everything in it. With her eyes closed she could pretend she was at home, in her own bed. She was worn out and, now she was warm, the urge to drop off for a few minutes was becoming irresistible.

She sank deeper into the sofa and was slumbering peacefully when she lolled sidewards and almost rolled off. Corbin jumped up, it must have looked as if she had fainted again, and she snapped with the irritability of a disturbed drowser, 'Sorry, I was asleep.'

'Nice to have an easy conscience,' he drawled.

'I was tired.'

'Then lie down and go to sleep. Get up.' He gestured her away from the sofa and pulled it out so that it made a bed.

With cushions and a travelling rug it was tempting, and she knew there was no need to ask, 'Where do you sleep?' although she did.

He said, 'Obviously not with you. There are other beds in other rooms.'

She said in a small voice, 'Then thank you very much.'

'You don't expect me to say, you're welcome?'

'I don't expect anything from you.'

'Don't bank on that, you can expect plenty.' He looked grim, and she glared at him.

'Make up your mind—do you want me to keep quiet or do you want a slanging match?'

'Go to sleep.'

'Is that the bathroom?'

There was only one inner door. Livvy was heading for it as he said, 'Yes.' The room was small and clinically white. Soap, towels and a toilet bag were the only signs that it was being used, but the water ran hot. A bath would have been nice. She would have to be in here for hours before he would knock and enquire if she was all right. He was probably putting her out of his mind so effectively that when she was out of sight he never gave her a second thought. She could soak or drown, and until he wanted to use the bathroom himself he would have forgotten she was in here.

There was nothing to stop her undressing and lying in the warm water, except that even behind a locked door she would feel vulnerable naked. He wouldn't touch her, he wouldn't look at her. There was no logic in her reasoning, but she wouldn't bath in here.

Anyhow, she was so weary she might slip under, so she washed hands and face instead, thinking that the shadows under her eyes this morning were nothing compared to the way she looked now. Black shadows and white face, like a miserable Harlequin, and although it didn't matter how she looked she wished it had been an old lipstick, not an old eyeliner, she had dropped into her jacket pocket in the car park.

There was no shutter at the little bathroom window, and the snow made a white shifting pattern on the opaque glass. Livvy noticed the catch was broken and wondered vaguely if the window could be forced open. If it could, she might come back some time and steal the sketch. But more likely she would get herself stuck, or if she did get in it wouldn't be here.

Corbin didn't look up when she went back, and she bit her lip, holding back a childish impulse to shout, Boo! Games he could do without, and so could she. She curled up on the sofa-bed, expecting to go out like a light. When she had been sitting upright she hadn't been able to keep her eyes open. She was just as tired now, but sleep eluded her, and for some reason it was harder to pretend she was somewhere else.

She could hear the typewriter, and music playing softly. When the typewriter stopped tapping he had to be writing or thinking or listening to the music, and she couldn't get his image out of her head. She was seeing him as clearly as if she was leaning over the back of the sofa watching him. Even with her hood over her ears she could hear the music, and she thought, it's jazz, that's what it is. So that's the kind of music he likes. It was a music she knew next to nothing about, and at least he was playing it quietly.

At first the typing and the music irritated her, but gradually she was relaxing, becoming drowsier. And for a little while, as she drifted on the edge of sleep, the sounds seemed almost reassuring. As if this was how things ought to be.

She slept soundly and she dreamed, and when she stirred again the lights were out. One bar of the gas fire kept the room warm and cast a glow, and she was still half asleep as she listened to the deep, steady breathing beside her. She said softly, 'Corbin?' and stretched out a hand.

She touched fur and shot upright, and so did Luke, growling and showing his teeth. When she shrieked he began to bark, and Corbin appeared at the top of the open staircase, while Livvy went on shrieking, 'Your dog gave me the shock of my life! Get him off my bed!'

'Whose bed?'

She threw the travelling rug aside and staggered to her feet. 'I shouldn't be here.'

'We're agreed on that.'

Luke, undecided where the emergency was, was rushing around the room barking his head off, and Livvy screamed, 'Shut up!'

'You shut up,' snapped Corbin. 'You're what's sending him crazy. He isn't used to women screaming in the middle of the night.'

She said, 'You surprise me—with you I'd have thought he might have been,' and that was a daft thing to say, but she had been shaken out of her wits. She opened the front door a crack, peered through and announced, 'It's stopped snowing.'

The wind was moaning now, rather than howling. There was no sign of moon or stars in the black sky, but the blanket of white covering everything threw up its own eerie light. 'I'm going,' she said.

She pulled on her boots and looked around for her mittens. She had slept in everything else, which hadn't been clever because the temperature outside was going to come as a savage shock.

Corbin closed the door, and when she turned towards it he said, 'As soon as dawn breaks.'

He was barelegged in that short navy towelling robe again, and Livvy faced him pugnaciously, muffled up to the eyebrows, muttering, 'Look, I know the way.'

'Sure,' he said. 'Down. And I did say you could drop off a cliff, but it's already been done and I haven't finished with that case yet, without starting on a did-she-fall-or-was-she-pushed on you.'

He turned the key and pocketed it, and she was not sorry; it would have been risky, but she felt compelled to protest. 'You've no right to keep me here!'

'Goodnight,' he said. 'What's left of it.'

He went up the wooden stairs with the dog at his heels, and she called after him, 'I could go through your bathroom window; the catch is broken.'

'Not unless you stripped off and greased yourself,' he said. 'Didn't you see the size of it? But if you're that set, go ahead, the butter's in the kitchen.'

As he shut the door up there Livvy said tartly, 'Thank you very much,' although he wouldn't hear her. It was common sense to wait for daylight before she started slithering down the hillside, but as soon as she could see her way she would be gone. She couldn't remember what she had been dreaming, but she knew she had expected to find him beside her when she woke, and those kind of dreams could destroy her.

It was being here that did it, shut in with somebody who ought to have been right but wasn't. But now she was wide awake and her defences were working again. Corbin Radbrook was the last man in the world she wanted to wake up with, and she was the last woman he wanted anywhere near him, and she wished she had slept longer so that there would have been less time to kill till morning.

She turned on another bar of the fire and the lamp by the window. She opened the shutters of the second window so that she would see when the sky started to lighten, then she went into the kitchen section where the black manual typewriter stood on the table. There were no files and no papers; of course, he wasn't leaving anything down here with her. Her head was aching a little so she opened the medicine cabinet fixed to the bathroom wall, but there wasn't even an aspirin.

He wouldn't need aspirins, he wouldn't have headaches, and if she knocked on his door and said, I suppose you don't have anything that would make me sleep, he would probably set the dog on her. Or should she start screaming again? That would get Luke barking; why should they sleep when she couldn't?

But if she did Corbin could put her outside, and at least she was warm in here. Going quietly mad, but warm. In the end she lay down on the sofa-bed and dozed again until she heard him coming down the stairs, and outside the window the sky was grey.

He let the dog out and went into the bathroom, and came out shaved and dressed, enquiring, 'Are you staying for breakfast?'

No more snow had fallen. The track was covered, but with a little caution she could get down. She said, 'No, thank you. What time can I tell Aunt Maysie to expect you?'

'I'll be right behind you. Not even coffee?'

She was standing at the window watching Luke racing up and down, and she said, 'All right, then.'

She stayed where she was until he said, 'Here you are.' Then she went across to pick up the cup of coffee from the kitchen table and carry it back to the window.

It was easier looking out, that way she didn't have to look at Corbin. There was no sense making things worse by carrying on slanging. If he spoke to her it would be cool and cutting, and that would be her attitude too, and yet part of her wanted to say, Don't hate me, because I don't think I'll ever be able to get you out of my mind.

At best he would laugh at her, without giving an inch; at worst he might say, When I've finished with you and yours, I guarantee you'll never forget me. So she stayed with her back to the room, gulping down the hot coffee, fighting that longing to go to him and look into his eyes whatever he said, to see if there was not something there that did not despise her.

They left the cottage at the same time and trudged down to the cars more or less together, not talking and not touching, but taking the track at the same pace. It was still freezing, but as they came down from the cliff top the carpet of snow was sparser, and Livvy walked carefully. She would not for the world have slipped. Corbin was not convinced she had fainted, and if she pitched over again it would be humiliating having to gather herself up under his ironic gaze.

But she wouldn't mind seeing him fall down. At least it might break the silence. What with the snow muffling everything, even Luke's snuffles as he padded along nose to the ground, this was like being on a cold lost planet.

Of course Corbin didn't tumble, and Livvy was sure the silence was not bothering him, but it was getting on her nerves so that she could have cheered at the sight of the frost-covered cars in the field.

She busied herself with hers, breathing on key and lock, warming both before she could open up. Then spraying and scraping the windows, and finally coaxing a chilled ignition into life. As she drove out of the field, Corbin's car followed her. 'Right behind you,' he had said, and he was a man of his word.

She saw him in her driving mirror and then she kept her eyes on the road ahead. She didn't need to see her own reflection to remind herself what a wreck she must look.

When she got back she would probably find somebody setting off to search for her. With the snow falling they would be bound to worry, and it had been a pretty near thing, she hadn't had much strength left when she had reached the cottage.

She hurried up the steps to the house, unlocking the door and leaving it ajar for Corbin to follow as she made straight for the kitchen. It was still early, that was where they were most likely to be. And so they were: Henry and Sonia and Daisy, with their breakfasts in front of them.

If they were worrying about Livvy it wasn't affecting their appetites. They all looked cheerful. Even Daisy was smiling at Corbin, who had walked into the room just behind Livvy. 'Morning,' said Henry.

Sonia said hello with a knowing leer, and Livvy said, 'Well, I got up there and the snow came.'

'That's what we thought,' said Henry, 'but we knew you'd be all right with Corbin.'

They thought there had been a blissful reconciliation in the little cottage while outside the snow swirled. Livvy said, 'It didn't occur to you that I could have been stuck half-way? It started snowing almost as soon as I started climbing.'

'If you set your mind to it, m'dear, you'd get up Everest!' chuckled Henry.

She supposed she was glad they hadn't been worrying, but they had too much faith in her stamina. She was not Superwoman. She muttered, 'It felt like bloody Everest.'

Henry gestured to the chair at the table. 'Come and sit down, my boy. Livvy will want to be popping up to see Maybelle.'

Livvy walked out of the kitchen, brushing past Corbin but not looking at him. By the time she had run up the two flights she had blinked away the angry tears. She should not have been angry and it was more like frustration, everybody insisting she was the strong one when she felt so unhappy and lonely. Everest? she thought as she opened the door and the cats came jumping at her, the way I feel now, I couldn't climb a molehill!

From the bedroom Aunt Maysie called, 'Have you brought Corbin back with you?'

'Yes,' said Livvy. 'What are you going to wear today?'

Maybelle made her selection and Livvy laid out her clothes. Then she said, 'I need a wash and a change myself,' and escaped to her own room to put on as good a face as possible for what lay ahead.

It was harder than usual. It needed skill to blot out the shadows and give herself a pretty mask to hide behind. At last, with colour on her lips and cheekbones, a touch of silver highlights, and her eyes given the full discreet treatment looking as blue as Schula's, she got up from the dressing-table.

The cat had followed her into the room and watched her get into a soft cream sweater, brown trousers and brown suede boots. Livvy had worn those the first time she had gone out with Corbin, and perhaps she was trying to put the clock back. The perfume he had given her was on the dressing-table, the only other bottle was that she had mixed from dregs, and she reached for his gift and sprayed it on. She might as well use it; she had used it last week and she could hardly hand it back now.

He was in Henry's room. The door was open and she heard Henry's voice. They were standing in the square tower window alcove with the mounted telescope swung towards the sea. Corbin was looking through it and Henry was informing him that the ship on the skyline was the QE2.

Henry said, 'Ah, here's Livvy,' but Corbin went on looking out to sea until she was standing beside them.

Then he said, 'She's a beauty,' meaning the telescope.

Livvy said, 'I watched you through that the first morning you came here. You stopped the car and you were looking back at the house and I wondered what you were thinking. Now I know.'

'Do you?'

'Maybelle Murrin lives there. How can I get her talking and what can she tell me?'

'And what can she?'

'She's waiting,' said Livvy, 'and you'd better go gently with her.'

'I see the colour's come back to your face.'

'I think it's more civilised to go down with colours flying,' she said, and when Henry chuckled she was as startled as though she had believed they were alone. She had to break free of this spell where Corbin could shut out everyone else, and she walked out of the room knowing they would both follow her.

Maybelle was sitting on the chaise-longue, smiling her enchanting smile. She welcomed Corbin as if he was a favourite caller, indicating where he should sit on the end of her sofa.

Tall, long-legged and devastatingly attractive, he lounged there, smiling and relaxed. Henry was sitting stiff-backed in his usual winged chair, and as Livvy seated herself Schula landed in her lap.

She began to stroke the cat, and Corbin turned from Maybelle to look across at her. The game was in his hands now, she had to play the cards he dealt her. It's you versus me, she was signalling, and his eyes took in the face of the girl, then the cat, both fixing him in a blue unblinking stare.

He said to Maybelle, 'You sent for me.'

'If I hadn't, you would have wanted to see me.'

'Very much.'

'You saw the sketch. Did you bring it with you?'

Livvy could have said, He'll say no, because you would ask for it back and it's his trump card. But she said nothing, and when Corbin said, 'I'm sorry,' Maybelle said,

'That was how he looked. You wanted to know that, didn't you? You want to know about him and I'm going to tell you, but in my own words and my own time.'

He nodded, and Livvy thought, no questions till later. He's too good a journalist not to have learned when to be quiet.

'He was almost as tall as you, and I think he was even more handsome,' Maybelle went on. 'He had grey eyes and he could smile so that I was the only one who knew he was smiling. He was fair-haired, and so was I—my hair was like Livvy's then.' She glanced at Livvy, but her eyes had a faraway look. 'That photograph at the garden party, that was the first time we met. I was with my friends and he was with his, and I felt him looking at me. I turned——' she turned her head away from them, 'and he was standing some distance away with quite a crowd between us, but we seemed to recognise each other as though we'd known each other all our lives.

'I was sailing to New York to marry Edward at the end of the year. We'd been engaged since I was twenty, I was twenty-three when I looked at Laurie and knew I was in love with him. And that he loved me. We hardly spoke, but we watched each other all afternoon, and it was better than talking because no one else could hear.'

She could have been talking to herself. Her glance drifted across them and her smile was the secretive smile of the girl in the sketch. 'No one else ever did hear, because I knew that if anyone else found out they would have made it ugly.

'We had a wonderful summer.' Now her face was radiant. 'Laurie flirted with other girls, but they meant nothing. He tried to make me jealous, but we always ended up laughing because I was so sure of him. And he was sure of me then.

'Mostly we met at night. It was a long, hot summer, and sometimes we met on the downs or on the beach. Sometimes he came here and sometimes I went to the cottage. He was painting for the exhibition—that painting wasn't one of his best. I remember them all, I could describe every one.

'And the cottage.' She was seeing Corbin now. 'The cottage will have changed?' He nodded. 'I can tell you how it was.'

She must have seen the painting of the Dark Lady, and Livvy waited for him to ask about that, but he didn't. Then Maybelle was saying, 'I was there the night he died.'

Livvy jerked forward, warning words trembling on her lips, but Corbin hushed her with a fierce gesture and Maybelle went on quietly, as if she was telling an old sad tale.

'I was sailing next day, but Laurie didn't believe I could marry anyone but him. He thought I was coming to the cottage that night to stay with him, and from then on everything would be out in the open. Our love should have been enough because nothing else in my life ever came near it, but that night other things seemed important. Like duty, and a promise to a man who had been waiting for me for years. But now I know that it was cowardice. Edward was security. Laurie and I had shared a summer madness. I was afraid. So I told him I was going to Edward, and that was how everything ended.'

Her eyes were blue-grey stones again. It had ended, she said, but none of them moved, because the story was not finished. Although, when Maybelle spoke again, her voice was flat and dead.

'He'd been drinking before I came. I'd never seen him drunk and he wasn't drunk then, but he must have had some idea what might happen, and while I was trying to explain he drained nearly half a tumbler of whisky.'

Livvy had heard the memories before of that last tortured meeting, but the jealousy had been Laurie's, not Maybelle's. His anger and accusations.

Maybelle said, 'He raced through the cottage and threw everything I'd ever given him into a bag. They were only little things: a scarf, a handkerchief, a book. He pulled open drawers and cupboards and he burned letters and notes on the stove, and he threw the painting from the top of the stairs.'

Then Corbin spoke for the first time. 'The Dark Lady?'

'You know,' agreed Maybelle.

He said, 'It was you?' and Livvy gasped.

'I was his Dark Lady of the night,' said Maybelle. 'His gypsy queen. He poured something on her until she looked like someone from hell. I couldn't bear to look and I ran away. It had been raining all day. There was a storm, I could have gone over the cliff, broken my neck like Laurie did. But I got here safely, still clutching the bag, and no one missed me.

'I left next morning, and Edward and I were married. When we came back from our honeymoon there were letters waiting. The news from home was that Laurie was dead.'

Corbin asked, 'Did Edward know?'

Maybelle said, 'He wasn't that perceptive, and I owed him peace of mind,' and Livvy wondered at the strength she would have needed. 'I made him happy,' she said softly. 'It wasn't hard because I loved him as he loved me for all the years we were together, but it was a different loving with Laurie. I would have been a different woman with him. In a way, my life ended that night too. I killed myself when I killed him, because it was my fault he died. He went out along the cliffs, and I don't know if it was an accident or if he meant to fall, but it was because of me he was there, it was because of me he died.'

Her voice trailed into silence, and Livvy whispered, 'So that was what you meant.'

They all looked at her, and she stammered, 'You said, "I killed Laurie," when you were delirious. I thought you were the one who was jealous. I thought there might have been a scuffle on the cliffs. I thought——' She gestured miserably.

Henry shook his head in disbelief before he exploded, 'You thought she *killed* a man? Livvy, you're no judge of character!'

'I can't be, can I? I wish you'd told me.'

'It was not a secret I wished to share,' Maybelle said quietly. 'What's the cottage like now?' She was asking Corbin, not Livvy, and as he began to describe it for her Livvy got up and slipped out of the room.

She might have offended Maybelle. It was one thing to feel morally responsible for a man's death, another when someone accepted without question that you had killed him with your own hands. Henry was shocked to the core. And nobody would understand what it had been like, listening to Maybelle in her fever. In all her distorted ravings, the only words she had spoken clearly were, 'Don't leave me,' and, 'I killed Laurie.'

And it was no more incredible than the passionate affair they had hidden from everyone through the hot summer till the winter storms; and the secrets that Maybelle had lived with ever since.

Livvy got her coat from her room, and when she reached the hall Sonia came hurrying up, asking, 'What's going on? Where are you going?'

'Don't ask me,' said Livvy. She walked past Sonia to where both cars still stood in the forecourt. She didn't think she would be going anywhere, but sooner or later Corbin would come out here and then she would talk to him.

She had no idea what she would say, but the words would surely come. She had been mistaken and she had acted stupidly, but there was nothing for them to fight about any more. She would apologise and hope they could be friends.

It was so cold. She shivered as she walked up and down, and when Luke barked from the car she went over and let him out. He wagged his tail and she said, 'We could get on all right, you and me, so long as you and the cats kept apart.'

The dog made for the front door and Livvy said, 'I can't let you in there, but he'll be coming. Run around and keep me company.'

Corbin came out of the house alone, and that should have made it easier. She wished she could go to him as Luke did. Not with the same rush as the dog, of course, but at least walk to meet him instead of standing rooted to the ground where she was; by the red brick wall that overlooked the garden.

He saw her, and she couldn't tell if he was surprised at finding her out here. From his expression she couldn't tell a thing. He looked across and saw her. He walked towards his car that was parked near, and just before he reached it she asked, 'Well, did you find it riveting?'

'Yes.'

She said in a rush, 'It was a relief to me. She said she killed him and I took that literally; that's why I was so frantic you were going to get a confession out of her.'

'Only to a love-affair.'

'I thought she killed him—I thought it might kill her if that was dragged out.'

Corbin said, 'I'm not a doctor, but I think she might be under less strain now,' and Livvy managed a little laugh.

'Well, I will.' The big fear should have been lifted, but she was still afraid because he was so distant.

He said drily, 'You've had a busy time since I turned up.' He opened the door for the dog, and was going to get in and drive away, and they hadn't talked at all.

She had to move. She went round the car and put a hand on his arm, asking, 'Can't we be friends?'

Her fingers tightened, but when he turned to shut the car door, keeping Luke in, somehow he shrugged her away. He said, 'This seems to be confession time,' and walked from her the few steps to the wall, and stood looking out over the snow-streaked garden.

Livvy stood beside him, and echoed, 'Confession?' arching her eyebrows and scared sick without knowing why.

'I mentioned the case that started me off in my line of journalism.' She nodded, but he wasn't looking at her. 'I was personally involved in that, and not as a lawyer but because the man was my best friend. The woman in his life seemed ideal for him, but she lied and she double-crossed and in the end she broke him. He couldn't see it until it was too late, but it taught me a lesson I should never have forgotten. I took no one at face value after that, and I thought I could spot a cheat anywhere.'

It wasn't the cold air that was making Livvy's face burn so that she was blushing to the roots of her hair, and Corbin didn't see that either. He said, 'You saw me stop and look back at the house after I'd met you for the first time. I wasn't thinking about Maybelle, I was thinking about you and what seemed to me then to have been the miracle of finding you.'

She nearly touched his arm again, to make him look at her, but his profile was as hard as a bronze statue's and she dared not touch him.

He said, 'For nearly ten years I've had good friends, and lovers, but I never lost my head over any of them. Only with you. I was blinded with you as though I'd known and trusted you all my life, and all the time you were playing me along.'

He turned to look at her then, and smiled, but she got no comfort from it. 'I don't blame you for that, Maybelle's all the family you have and your concern for her does you credit. But you're too good at acting, my pretty.

'If you like, we're friends. I'm sure you have plenty of friends, but don't put me too high on the list. Don't count on me and don't call me.'

A friend who was no friend. Livvy could never think of him that way. She said, 'That's how you want it?'

'That's how it is.'

He had said it had been like a miracle in the beginning, and although his mind was rejecting her now the physical pull could still be working. When she was touching him she could go up in flames, and he had to feel it too. The force was so fierce between them.

She moved very close, her face raised to his. 'Kiss me goodbye,' she said.

He looked down at her and she willed with all her might that the hard face would soften—a reluctant smile tug the corner of his mouth, a lift of an eyebrow. Any crack in the armour that would give her hope. But when he said, 'Don't be ridiculous,' there was no tenderness in his voice.

Nor in the face. No anger either, just something that told her this was really goodbye and that there would never again be a place in his life for her.

CHAPTER EIGHT

LIVVY watched the car drive away and wondered if this was how Maybelle had felt, as if all hope of happiness had gone from her. Sixty years on would Livvy be saying, I would have been a different woman with him, it would have been a different life?

But there would be no second-best for Livvy. No Edward, no Andrew either. Nobody but Corbin, and somehow she must get him back, because without him it would be no life. Panic could have started her running after his car and once more climbing the hill to the cottage, and that would have been madness when he was so relentlessly set against her.

She had to believe that somehow, some time, it would come right, or she could start screaming and never stop. But in her heart she knew that she could have killed everything Corbin felt for her as surely as Maybelle had believed she'd killed Laurie.

She walked with fast, long strides from the house, taking the cliff road that led towards the town, not the chine and the cottage. Traffic was almost nil, just the occasional car until she was almost in town. Andrew was down there, and so were friends she had known all her life.

She could call on them and count on them, but not with this problem. I'm in love for the first time in my life with a man I cheated. He doesn't care for cheats, so what do I do now? How do I make him trust me and love me so that he'll never want any other woman as long as we both shall live?

152

'That,' she said aloud, 'is a tall order, as if we're still talking of Everest,' and a sob rose in her throat. But sobbing would be as useless as screaming. She had to be calm and she had to go home, and she stood for a while, forcing control. She could have fallen apart, but she held herself rigid and a chill seemed to spread through her, starting in her heart, until her whole body felt numb, and deadened, then she turned and retraced her steps, jogging now so that she got back even faster than she had come.

Sonia met her in the hall, asking, 'Where have you been?'

'Walking,' said Livvy, which was no answer, but Sonia was too excited to notice.

'How about it? Aunt Maysie and Laurence Charles! Good friends, Henry says, and she's going to tell Corbin all about him and even what the cottage was like. Were they *very* good friends?'

'Very,' said Livvy, and Sonia smiled and sighed.

'Isn't it romantic? You knew?'

'Yes.'

'Aren't you the deep one? And you kept it from Corbin?'

'Not for long. He knows now.'

'Well, he would, wouldn't he?' said Sonia. 'There's not much you could hide from a man like him.'

'Not much,' Livvy agreed as she went up the stairs to face Henry on the first landing. Probably he had been waiting for her too, but he was not smiling. In Henry's eyes till now Livvy had been able to do no wrong. Now he said in sorrow and anger, 'I cannot believe you could believe a thing like that about Maybelle.'

'I got it wrong,' said Livvy. 'How is she?'

'Remarkably composed, everything considered.' Henry gave her a no-thanks-to-you glare. 'Remarkable woman.'

'So you keep saying,' said Livvy. She tapped on Maybelle's door and called, 'May I come in?'

'Of course,' Maybelle called back. 'Why do you ask?'

Livvy had always walked into Maybelle's apartment without knocking. Now she said, 'I won't be barging in on Henry without permission for a while. I'm about as welcome as Daisy was when she let the dog out.'

Maybelle laughed and was grave again immediately, asking, 'What did I say?'

She meant on the night of her fever. Livvy went and sat by her on the chaise-longue and said quietly, 'You said, "Don't leave me, Laurie", but you left him.'

'Not as he left me,' said Maybelle. 'I was still somewhere in the world. Dear Livvy,' she said a moment later, 'did I frighten you?'

Livvy said, 'I was afraid you were dying. You were delirious and something that happened a long time ago was burning up your brain, and when you said, "I killed Laurie", I was glad there was no one else to hear. That would have frightened me. So long as I was the only one who knew, you were safe. I didn't know who Laurie was that night and I didn't care. All I wanted to do was keep you alive.

'Later I found the sketch and the photograph in the chest, and I knew then that he was Laurence Charles, but no one else would ever have known if I'd let you burn the sketch. That was my mistake. If Corbin hadn't seen that, none of this would have happened.'

Maybelle said softly, 'I'm glad you didn't burn it, although I never wanted you to know. Not because I was ashamed of loving Laurie, but because I was so weak at the end. He had such promise and it was all wasted. All his gifts, all his talent.'

Livvy said, 'It was an accident,' and she was convinced it was. 'A tragedy, but an accident.'

'That was what Corbin said. I've never spoken about Laurie all these years, and now I must.'

It seemed that Corbin was right again. The strain of secrecy was lifted after a lifetime of silence, and Livvy knew she would tell Corbin about that golden summer, and instead of harming her it could give her a new lease of life. 'What happens now?' she asked Maybelle.

'Corbin will be back tomorrow.' Maybelle sounded as if she was looking forward to it. 'You're glad he's coming back, aren't you?' Livvy shrugged, and Maybelle said pleadingly, 'Don't be proud. Don't lose him. I knew from the way he looked at you that first morning that there was something special between you.'

There was nothing between them now. Outside Corbin had looked at her as though she was nothing. Livvy said, 'We're friends,' and even that was not true. But it satisfied Maybelle, who went smiling to her writing desk, where Livvy left her making notes from her memories.

Henry was in the hall, waiting for Livvy. 'Those TV folk Corbin mentioned. He's getting in touch and asking a couple to come down—friends of his. Can we put them up?'

She asked, 'And Corbin?'

'He'll be staying on at the cottage.'

She pondered. 'It would mean opening bedrooms and putting on meals, and Christmas is nearly on us. Would they want to come before Christmas?'

'If the weather holds. Two rooms for two days.'

Henry wanted them here, and when she said, 'All right,' he smiled.

He was still shocked that she had so maligned Maybelle, but he could not stay angry with her for long. 'Should be interesting chaps,' he said. 'Friends of Corbin's—bound to be.'

Getting ready for them would keep Livvy busy, and the last thing she needed was time to brood. As it happened she was fully occupied for the rest of that day, because Sonia suggested, 'Shouldn't we start putting up the decorations if we're getting some paying guests?'

Around this time they would have started anyway. Decorating the parlour where they had the 'family' festivities, and the hall and the drawing-room for the Christmas party.

So Livvy climbed up into the attics, handing down cardboard boxes of glittering baubles and tinsel garlands. Most of them had been used for years, but they still came up fresh and bright, and Daisy was as ecstatic as though the treasures of Aladdin's cave were being spilled out before her.

Maybelle came downstairs and she and Henry supervised, remembering between them where everything ought to be, from the Chinese lanterns to the crib of small carved wooden figures; and directing Livvy and Sonia— 'No, dear, not the silver cascade there, the gold one. We always have the gold one over that window.'

Livvy and Sonia smiled at each other at the top of ladders. 'What would happen if we changed the pattern?' Sonia whispered. Livvy whispered back, 'Maysie would hook them down with her stick.'

But when they all stood back and looked around, Sonia said happily, 'It does look smashing, doesn't it?'

A silver tree, seven foot tall, had pride of place in the hall. There had always been a real fir tree until the year a pine needle embedded in a cat's paw turned septic and Maybelle had bought the silver tree. This had been erected for the last five years, gifts piled around, and hung about with scarlet baubles and fairy-lights.

Everything looked, as Sonia said, smashing, and Daisy, enchanted by the tiny Babe in the tiny manger, breathed, 'Christmas has really started now, hasn't it?'

'Shall I get some holly and mistletoe in the morning?' said Sonia.

Corbin arrived in the afternoon, when there was a holly wreath on the door and holly in a bronze bowl on the hall table. And a bunch of mistletoe hanging high over the foot of the stairs.

Sonia opened the door to him as Livvy came into the hall. He did a double-take at all the glitter, then he said, 'I like it.'

'Brightens the old place up,' said Livvy.

'Where will you be at Christmas?' asked Sonia.

'With friends.'

Sonia pouted. 'Aren't we your friends?'

'Of course you are,' he said promptly, looking up at the tree and the mistletoe. 'Mistletoe?'

'You must know about mistletoe,' Sonia simpered.

'You don't see much of it these days.'

'But it's traditional,' said Sonia.

'Of course it is.' He scooped up Daisy, who squealed with delight, and kissed the tip of her nose, and Sonia skipped up to them as he set Daisy down. When he kissed Sonia she put her arms around his neck, and Livvy thought, don't make a meal of it.

She walked past them on to the staircase. Aunt Maysie was waiting for him and that was why he was here, there was nothing for him to hang around down here for. When he moved from Sonia, Livvy went up another step and laughed and said, 'Not until Christmas.'

'When I won't be here.'

'Ahh!' she said in exaggerated regret. 'Well, I'll try to bear up.'

'And you will,' he said.

As he followed her she said, 'I hear we're expecting your colleagues.'

'The executive producer and the film producer of the series, if you can put them up.'

'When?'

'Next Tuesday. Two rooms for two nights.'

'I think we can manage that. So long as they don't need much waiting on.'

'It will be a working break. They want to look around the area.'

'And meet Maybelle?'

'She is the star of the script. Have you any objections?'

When they started on the second staircase, Livvy was still a couple of steps ahead. Speaking without turning to look at Corbin, she said, 'You were right. Now there's nothing to hide any more, she wants to talk about him.'

As she reached to open the door he was suddenly beside her and it was his hand on the doorknob. He said, 'I'd prefer to see her alone. You might cramp her style.'

'*What?*'

'It seems you have done for years.'

Livvy said sharply, 'Are you trying to be funny?'

'When you're around,' he said, 'I don't feel much like laughing.'

She said, 'Don't try. It's all been a rotten joke. As Henry says, I must be a lousy judge of character, casting Maybelle as a killer.'

'I wasn't too sharp myself. Both of us blind as bats.'

'One little thing we did have in common.'

'And damn all else.'

'Right,' she said. 'Apart from that small error of judgement you always are right, aren't you? It must be lovely to be always right.'

He opened the door and asked, 'May I come in?' and closed it on Livvy when Maybelle answered.

She nearly marched in after him. How dared he slam a door on her in her own house? Much more of this and she would be well on the way to resenting him. He was an arrogant so-and-so, and she was not too infatuated to see that.

Downstairs, Sonia was starry-eyed. 'He kissed me!'

Livvy said, 'He's very good at it.'

'Why didn't you let him kiss you?'

'Because he's too good at it. I didn't want him sweeping me off my feet.'

'You *are* joking?'

'Of *course*.' But she was not, although she burst out laughing and Sonia laughed with her.

When the house was quiet that night and they were all asleep, Livvy gathered the presents Corbin had given her from her bedroom and climbed up with them into the attics.

Some time she would give them away in their turn, but that would be after he had left the Island. Meanwhile she put them in an old cabin trunk under the eaves in the shadows, well away from the dusty, swinging light bulb, and that was being sensible.

After her panic when Corbin had driven away she was being sensible. What can't be cured must be endured, she decided. She could never change what had happened. She had to carry on and keep very busy.

In the following days, the build-up to Christmas gained impetus, with Livvy catching up on things she would have done before if Corbin had not been occupying so much of her time—sending cards, buying gifts. The weather varied from cold enough for snow to an unseasonably warm couple of days when the ice melted and the trees dripped and the ground was soggy.

In Sweet Orchard, Livvy stacked her decorating paint and paper, brushes and ladders, into one room, where they would remain until the festivities were over and the new year had begun.

Daisy was getting her mother to write lists for Father Christmas which grew longer every day and had Sonia worried. Henry had forgiven Livvy, although he still could not understand how she could have been so stupid, and Maybelle was blooming.

She looked fitter than she had for years, as if reliving her youth was stirring more than memories, brightening her eyes and smoothing her skin.

Corbin brought the tape recorder. They talked into it while he was here. Sometimes he left it behind, and Livvy knew that Maybelle played it back and talked to it herself. After Christmas, when things had quietened down, she would say, 'May I hear it?'

She would want to see the finished script, but it would mean asking Corbin if he minded. She had no legal right to be censoring anything, and right now everybody seemed to be having a good time. When the men who were responsible for the actual filming arrived she would talk to them, but Corbin did not want her around while he was interviewing, and there was always something else she should be doing.

As long as Livvy could remember, Sweet Orchard had been open house on Christmas Eve, when the same friends and neighbours came from midday until early evening, and although Livvy and Sonia were professional caterers the buffet needed organising and preparing. Most of the invitations were word of mouth— 'We'll see you on Christmas Eve, won't we?'—but some had to be sent along with Christmas cards, and everyone on the list had to be contacted in some way.

Corbin would not be here for Christmas, but Maybelle and Henry and Sonia kept inviting him. Livvy did not. She knew it was a waste of time, although he was here most days. Everyone else in the house saw no difference in him and he hadn't changed to them. He chatted with them, listened to them, but Livvy knew that no one really got near him.

The magic circle that had once surrounded her and Corbin had gone, together with all the warmth and the closeness that could have kept her young for ever. She was an outsider now, like the others, because Corbin Radbrook was a self-contained man who needed nobody.

What he felt for her was indifference, although she sometimes caught a weary cynicism in his expression when he looked at her; as if he blamed himself for being cheated as much as he blamed her, accepting the whole thing as a very closed chapter.

She would have done better to leave him alone, but for the life of her she couldn't. Like a moth to the flame she had to keep circling him, because while he was in the house she was drawn to him. She usually kept out of the way while he was talking to Maybelle, but when he was downstairs they often came across each other.

She was on the phone ticking off the party list, when he leaned over her shoulder to remark on its length. 'So many friends!' Then, with a gleam of cold amusement in his eyes, 'And I can't think of anyone who deserves friends more. I see Andrew's near the top of the list.'

Livvy raised wide eyes. 'The friends I can count on are.'

'Touché,' he said, and ran a light fingertip down her cheek in what might have looked like a caress but felt like the flick of a duelling foil.

She was really starting to dislike him, and maybe that was the best thing she could do for herself. Aversion therapy. Telling herself, every day I like him less. When she couldn't stand the sight of him, she would surely stop reaching for him in the night.

During the day it was easy, because he certainly did not like her, but alone in her room and her bed, when she was too weary to fight, he invaded her dreams, overwhelming her defences.

In her dreams, he was king and he worshipped her, so it was going to take time, and she had only a few days when his friends arrived.

They were coming to the Island by helicopter and Corbin was bringing them to Sweet Orchard, but Livvy was not there to welcome them because she had gone to town and been held up.

When she saw Corbin's car in the forecourt she parked her own and hurried into the kitchen and went towards the drawing-room, where she could hear voices through the open door.

Everybody else had rallied to meet the visitors. Aunt Maysie was presiding from the chair with the footstool. Henry stood in front of the fireplace, Daisy was carefully carrying teacups and Sonia was pouring from the silver teapot.

A man and a woman were the centre of attention. He was stocky and balding, with a moustache and an affable air. She was petite, pretty, silver-haired and something of a surprise to Livvy, who had expected two men, although Corbin had not specified that.

She started apologising, 'I'm sorry I'm late—I'm Livvy Murrin.'

Out of the corner of her mouth Sonia muttered, 'You ain't seen nothing yet!'

Corbin was not here. Henry stepped forward and launched into introductions. 'This is Hedley Higgins, executive producer—that's right, isn't it? And Mrs Higgins.'

The silver-haired woman said, 'Valerie.' She had a sweet smile, and Livvy asked, 'Are you the film producer?'

Valerie dimpled then. 'Goodness, not me! I hitched a ride at the last minute, I'm here for a little holiday. Anne-Marie's with Corbin, she's the film producer. Anne-Marie Benoit.'

Sonia said ruefully, 'And Anne-Marie's gorgeous,' and both the Higginses smiled.

'Isn't she just?' said Valerie, and Livvy felt as if she had been kicked in the stomach.

Somehow she managed to carry on saying the right things. She had had years of practice welcoming strangers into her home, and she asked them if this was the first time they had been to the Island—it was—and where they usually holidayed, which was abroad in the sun. When all she wanted to ask was, Where are Corbin and this gorgeous Anne-Marie, and what are they doing?

It could only have been a few minutes, although it seemed much longer to Livvy, before Corbin and the girl came into the room. When they did walk in, Livvy was the only one who didn't immediately look towards the door.

She had to look up, of course, and she wished she could have gone on staring into her teacup, because this was a woman who should have been in front of the cameras, not behind them. She was taller than Livvy, with a model's figure, a golden tan and a mass of flame-coloured hair. Her hand was through Corbin's arm. 'So you're Livvy,' she said, and smiled with a flash of perfect teeth.

Corbin must have been talking about her. Livvy's own face felt like a grinning mask. 'And you're Anne-Marie. How do you do, I'm delighted to meet you.'

She got up and went towards them, and she had never been less thrilled to meet anybody.

'Well, it's a pretty room you've got for me,' Anne-Marie was saying, 'but I'm afraid I won't be using it. Corbin thinks I should be staying in the cottage. We'll be filming in there and I want to get the atmosphere, the feel of the place.'

The Higgins exchanged amused glances and Hedley said, 'Oh, yes, you should be getting the feel of the place. Big enough for two, is it?'

'Sleeps six in the summer season,' said Corbin, and Hedley grinned.

'Well, you'll excuse us if we don't join you. We think we might be more comfortable here.'

'We'll excuse you,' said Corbin, and Hedley guffawed.

'I thought you would!'

They went on joking, talking, taking tea, and Livvy was as lively as anyone—although she felt like a walking doll, as if everything about her was working mechanically.

It was a merry little party, and when Livvy murmured, 'Excuse me, something I have to see to,' and slipped out of the room, she doubted if anyone really noticed. Sitting with Corbin on a sofa, Anne-Marie was leaning on his shoulder.

Livvy went through the hall into the study, and sat down at the desk and cradled her aching head on her folded arms. Jealousy was raging in her, and she thought, I could have been right about Aunt Maysie, she could have killed the man she loved. I hate that girl so much. And I hate Corbin. I could kill them! Or myself. How am I going to get through the nights, knowing they're sleeping together? Or even the days, when they're working together?

She shot upright as Sonia walked in. 'Are you all right?' Sonia asked.

Livvy heard herself say, 'It was rather a shock.' Like lightning striking and shrivelling you to a crisp.

Sonia came to the desk, her face puckered with pity. 'He was alone here, but there had to be other women— we always knew that, didn't we?'

'Yes, we always knew.'

A man with Corbin's charisma would only have to walk into a crowded room and there would be women in his life if he wanted them. But Livvy had never seen him with a woman he wanted before. She had even been jealous of Sonia, but he and Anne-Marie were lovers, and the thought of that hurt like something sharp and cutting inside her.

Sonia said mournfully, 'It isn't fair! She's got everything. She makes you look like nothing, so what does she make me look like?'

'Less of a fool than me,' said Livvy.

'You did fancy him, didn't you?'

'Yes.' Too much to find words to describe it.

'She's got everything!' Sonia wailed again. 'I suppose they're really the perfect pair.' She was not being bitchy— it was true. She asked, 'What are you going to do?'

'Keep out of the way.' She couldn't hold a candle to Anne-Marie for looks, nor for brains when it came to the work that had brought her here. While Anne-Marie was on the Island they would be inseparable, Livvy knew that, but she could not hang around to watch.

She said, 'If anybody asks, I'm in the kitchen, seeing to the dinner.' A meal had to be prepared, one of their regular à la carte menus that Livvy and Sonia had produced hundreds of times and that she could almost have cooked blindfold.

She was blending an avocado cream dressing when Sonia turned up again and said, 'Valerie's a vegetarian.'

'That's no problem,' said Livvy.

'And two less.' Sonia sounded like the bearer of bad news. 'Corbin and Anne-Marie are going, they want to get up to the cottage before it gets dark.'

'Two less,' said Livvy.

'Well, it's quite a climb and it's slippery, what with the frost and all, although I suppose she can always hang on to Corbin.' She bit her lip and stuttered, 'Sorry, that wasn't what I meant to say,' and Livvy forced a smile.

'Sure she will. She was leaning on him in the drawing-room just now as if she needed support,' and Sonia giggled.

'You'd think she could support herself, wouldn't you, a big strong girl like her.' It wasn't funny, but both girls laughed, and Sonia said, 'Oh, I'm glad you're laughing.'

'If you've got to lose,' said Livvy, 'you might as well smile about it.'

'Oh, *yes*!' Sonia said fervently, and Livvy poured the dressing into a small tureen while Sonia went back to the drawing-room. Livvy was not a good loser, she was a rotten loser, but she was not dragging her friends and her family down into her own depths of despair.

She sat through dinner that night with Sonia and Henry and Maybelle and Mr and Mrs Higgins, and was a gay and charming hostess. The Higginses said the food was delicious, and afterwards they made up a four for bridge with Henry and Maybelle.

Livvy chattered on the phone and wrapped some of the gifts she had bought in town that afternoon, ticking them off her list and writing out name tags. And once or twice she caught herself frowning at the name she was writing because she couldn't put a face to it. These were people she had known all her life and they hardly seemed real any more.

It was as though she was only half awake, but she carried on doing the things she had to do and finding the right words when she had to speak. Saying good-night to Maybelle was no picnic, because Maybelle had seen how things were with Corbin and Anne-Marie. Livvy hadn't seemed to mind too much. She had seemed in good spirits, but when she came into Maybelle's apartment last thing Maybelle was sitting up in bed, waiting for her.

'All right, dear?' Maybelle enquired.

'Yes,' said Livvy. 'They're a nice couple, aren't they?'

'They were saying,' said Maybelle, 'at least, Valerie was—that Anne-Marie's been after Corbin for a long time. She said she isn't going to miss a chance like this.'

'Good luck to her,' said Livvy.

'I did hope you and he——' Maybelle began, and Livvy smiled. It was easy to smile, you just stretched your lips and kept your voice light and steady.

'We're friends, but there was never anything more.'

She kissed Maybelle's cheek and Maybelle said, 'If you say so,' and because she wanted to believe that Livvy's heart was not aching she probably did.

Schula knew. She padded behind Livvy into her bedroom, curling up on the duvet, and Livvy lay in the dark stroking the cat. She had thought she would be caught up in a storm of weeping as soon as she relaxed, but her eyes were dry and the ache was more of a dull emptiness.

She wouldn't think about the cottage, or Corbin and the girl who had beauty and brains and everything else, because that would be like tearing a wound open. So long as she could block them out the pain was blocked too.

It was the first night she did not dream of Corbin. She was sure of that, although she didn't think she had dreamed of anything. She woke and remembered Anne-Marie, and right away, like a whiff of anaesthetic, the numbness took over.

Downstairs she faced them all, the family first, then the Higginses, with a cheerfulness that looked natural. She kept out of the way when Corbin and Anne-Marie arrived to collect Hedley and Valerie, and during the day Livvy and Sonia, and Daisy in a small way, worked on the party fare, laying out plates and cutlery and glasses for the buffet.

There was a grim moment that evening when Hedley and Anne-Marie and Corbin were discussing possible actors for the programme. They had been out all day—Anne-Marie and Corbin were going on somewhere else for dinner—but now they were all in the drawing-room and Livvy and Sonia were pouring out coffee or sherry.

Hedley had just taken a large sherry when he said, 'It's a shame we can't offer you the part of the young Maybelle, Livvy.'

'*What?*' Livvy almost scalded herself with a stream of coffee that splashed into the saucer, and Hedley went on,

'You're very like Miss Murrin must have been. You never have acted professionally?'

Livvy said, 'I've never acted at all.'

'I don't believe that,' said Corbin. 'You'd make a brilliant actress, you're a natural.'

'What makes you think so?' Anne-Marie looked Livvy up and down as if she was auditioning her and was not impressed.

'A gut reaction,' replied Corbin.

'Well, it can't be done,' said Anne-Marie. 'Equity wouldn't wear it.'

'No, thank you,' said Livvy.

She knew that Corbin was laughing at her and that he had meant to embarrass her, and she wondered if he would explain to Anne-Marie tonight and if she would enjoy the joke.

Next day was Christmas Eve, and guests were expected from midday. It was a shame that Hedley and Valerie, and Anne-Marie and Corbin, could not stay on a few hours more and join in the party. But after breakfast the helicopter was air-lifting the three of them and they had their own Christmas schedules arranged. Corbin was taking them to the helicopter pad, then driving into Cowes and joining friends there, and Livvy dodged him and Anne-Marie until the very last minute.

The Higginses had had breakfast and were packed and ready. It had been a short stay but an excellent recce, Hedley said, giving him a good idea how they were going to handle the filming. Very rewarding, very worth while, and Sweet Orchard was the kind of place he and Valerie would definitely be putting on their holiday list.

When Corbin's car drew up, Valerie was talking to Livvy, so that there was no way Livvy could run without making herself conspicuous as Corbin and Anne-Marie came into the hall.

Corbin carried parcels which he deposited with the piles around the tree, and Sonia said, 'Daisy and I have got something for you.'

It was wrapped in gold paper and it was a tie. She had shown it to Livvy and Livvy had said, 'Lovely,' and known that Corbin would never have chosen it.

Livvy had nothing for him, and she looked at the package that was obviously a painting for Maybelle, and wondered if it was a Laurence Charles, and the square bottle shape for Henry that looked like his awful rum.

Daisy's was a large box and Livvy's and Sonia's were flat, identical packs.

Anne-Marie smiled, 'I hope you two girls like them. I bought them for you yesterday.'

'Thank you,' they chorused.

'One for the road,' said Anne-Marie, looking up at the mistletoe.

There was kissing all round amid a flurry of farewells, but Corbin did not kiss Livvy, and she kept back, making sure he didn't. Then they trooped out to the car. 'See you after Christmas,' said Corbin, picking up Valerie's bag.

Anne-Marie hesitated for a final glance at the tree, so that for a moment she was alone in the hall with Livvy. 'I'm really enjoying myself here,' she said.

'I'm so glad,' said Livvy, lying and smiling.

Anne-Marie's smile was brilliant. 'It's such a dear little house that I can't bear to leave it, so we'll be going back there when we've dumped Hedley and Val.' Livvy could not think why she was being told this until Anne-Marie said very softly, 'All by ourselves for Christmas—can you think of anything nicer?'

She had gone, hurrying out to the car, before Livvy could answer. Not that there was much Livvy could have said. Anne-Marie must know how she felt. She might have guessed. Corbin might have said something that had raised her suspicions, and she meant Livvy to know how it was with her and Corbin.

I knew anyway, Livvy thought, and soon my friends will start arriving and I won't have time to care.

It was all go from then on. While she had been cooking and serving breakfast and hurrying through the chores, Livvy had worn a cover-all smock over her party get-up of silver shirt and swirling black chiffon skirt. She took off the smock now and spent a few minutes retouching her make-up, with plenty of blusher to liven up her pale face before she came down again to greet the early comers.

From midday the downstairs rooms were filled. Everybody who had been invited came and most of them stayed, because the buffet and the fruit punch bowl and the sparkling wines were as good as ever, and because they all knew each other. They were among friends and they had plenty to talk about.

Livvy was kissed under the mistletoe and told how lovely she looked, as she moved around making sure everybody was happy. When she was asked about Corbin, she said, 'Oh, he'll be back after Christmas.'

They wanted to hear about the visit of the TV people and the film that was planned around here, and Maybelle said, 'There'll be some surprises, I believe,' but would not be drawn further. Henry and Sonia said everyone would have to wait and see. They were enjoying their secret, but Livvy moved away every time she heard Corbin's name.

She kept out of it. She kept the dishes and glasses filled and she smiled a lot, and most of the time Andrew was with her.

Part of the fun was the presents. There were small gifts for all the guests from the piles under the tree, and most had brought tokens for the family. Family gifts were held back until Christmas Day, but Sonia came up to Livvy and Andrew with the two packets Corbin had left for them and said, 'I couldn't help it, I had to see what Anne-Marie got us.'

She had opened hers and handed Livvy the other pack, urging, 'Go on, see if yours is the same.'

It was a long-sleeved thermal vest. 'Snap,' said Sonia.

'She could have picked the lacy sort. She must think we lead chilly lives,' said Livvy.

'I'm beginning to think you do too,' said Andrew. 'It's the first time I've been kissed by an icicle.'

Andrew had kissed Livvy twice as they passed under the mistletoe. She had hardly felt his lips on hers, and she joked now, 'What do you expect, under the eyes of the whole neighbourhood?'

But there was something in her eyes that troubled him, and he said, 'I suppose you do remember we're going to Rob Wilson's?'

A man who worked with Andrew was giving a party this evening, and Livvy and Andrew had been invited ages ago. She had forgotten, although she said quickly, 'Of course. When should we be leaving?'

It was after six o'clock. Guests usually left here around seven.

'Any time now,' said Andrew, 'I did remind you yesterday.' His sarcasm was heavy. 'You do remember I rang you yesterday?'

'Of course.' She remembered that. 'You can cope, can't you?' Sonia nodded. 'Leave the wreckage till I get back,' said Livvy.

They went out through the kitchen, and on the way she took an anorak out of a cloaks cupboard and a small, flat torch out of a dresser drawer.

There was moonlight tonight in a sky of stars. It was cold and still, a waiting world, and Andrew led the way to his car, parked among the others in the forecourt. Some guests were leaving, but Livvy followed close behind Andrew and was in his car before they spotted her.

He turned on the heater, but it was still cold and the windows were misted, so she wound the passenger window down and up to clear it and wiped the windscreen with a tissue, then sat back in her seat, watching the landscape slide by. But she was not really watching, any more than she was listening to Andrew rabbiting on. They were driving towards Andrew's friend's flat in the direction of the cottage which was up there, where Corbin and Anne-Marie were all by themselves for Christmas.

So what am I doing *here*? Livvy thought, jolted suddenly as if she was waking from a deep sleep. I don't know what to do, but I surely know where I want to be.

She swivelled in her seat and looked blankly at Andrew. Not here, not with him, and he said resentfully, 'You're not listening. You don't hear me these days, you don't even see me.'

She was seeing him now; his blunt, pleasant features were mottled and screwed up, and she said, 'I'm sorry.'

'Do you want to come with me?'

There was only one answer. 'No.' And he slammed on the brakes so that they lurched forward in their seat-belts.

'You want me to take you back? You want to get out?'

Livvy unclicked her belt. 'I'll get out.'

'What's *happening* to you?' He hadn't expected her to jump from the car, but she did.

She said, 'Whatever it is, I don't think there's a cure.'

She ran up on to the lower slope of the hillside and he couldn't have caught her. She had always been fleet-footed, and if he did catch her, what could he say? She was fey, was Livvy. It was part of her charm. He wished he could catch her and keep her, but it seemed that almost before he could get out of the car and stare up and down and wonder what the hell to do, she had vanished. She didn't look back, and if he had shouted her name she would not have heard him.

This was another way up to the cottage, a longer climb than up from the meadow but easier than last time, because there was no wind and no snow. Livvy wrapped her anorak around her and her shoes were light but flatties, and she had the moonlight and the little torch.

Corbin was up in the cottage and Corbin must listen to her. 'I brought you a Christmas present,' she would say. 'All those presents you gave me over the years and I never gave you anything. We've known each other for years, haven't we? Didn't you know that, Anne-Marie? Oh, we go back a long way, he and I.'

When she saw the lamp burning, she stopped for a moment. They were there. She had known that, and that she would have to face them both and that it could be the worst humiliation of her life, but there was no way she was turning back.

'Don't be proud,' Maybelle had said, and Livvy was too proud to let Corbin walk off without counting the cost. They had nearly had a miracle going for them, and he had to know what he was throwing away.

He must listen. He must know. She knocked on the door and held her breath. No one answered, although the lamp was burning in the window. When she peered in, the room seemed empty, and that could mean they were upstairs and she cringed at the thought. But if they were she was getting them down.

She fairly beat on the door, but there was no answering sound, and surely Luke would have been barking by now, she was making din enough to wake the dead. So they were out, eating maybe, but coming back. And she could either walk down to where the car would be parked eventually or sit on the doorstep and freeze. Or break a window.

Livvy went round to the back of the cottage and looked at the bathroom window with the faulty catch. The catch might have been repaired, or the whole thing could be stuck tight. She dragged a piece of rock underneath and perched on top and began banging with her fist around the window-frame edges.

'That's more like it,' she said to herself when the window swung inwards. It was a small aperture, but she was slim and supple and, rid of her outer bulk, she might get through. She took off her coat, putting it on the ground, and on top of it her flowing skirt. She pulled herself up on to the ledge and squirmed.

The window was a very tight fit. She needed to gyrate in it like a belly dancer, twisting and turning, her shirt rumpling up her back and her skin getting scraped. For several horrible seconds she was stuck, but finally she jerked through, landing in the bath and lying there puffing for a few seconds more.

She had to get her skirt back at least, and she came out into the living-room. It was quite warm here, as well as the window lamp, a bar of the fire was burning, but they were out of the house because the door was locked, not bolted, and the key had gone. She was not climbing out again, so she had to fish for her clothes, and in the cupboard in the kitchenette was a broom that might do the job.

It was far from ideal. She could hook them with it, but she couldn't actually lift them in. She got her skirt almost up to the window and then it slid off, maddeningly farther away than ever. And the anorak was too heavy to manoeuvre. It was like a crazy game. Livvy was leaning out as far as she could, scooping them up and seeing them fall and getting more and more frustrated; and she might have to get out again and throw them in, then go through all the performance of climbing back. But she was not sure she could manage that right now, breathless and shivering like this.

By now she had scattered both skirt and coat out of reach, so she shut the window, sitting on the side of the bath, trying to get her breath back.

She heard Luke barking and looked wildly at the window. But there was no time to escape, and she heard Corbin's voice. She jumped up to lock the bolt on the bathroom door as Luke beat her to it, bursting in and flinging the door wide.

CHAPTER NINE

SEEING LIVVY, the dog stopped barking and stood there wagging his tail, and she thought crazily, he's glad to see me, things are looking up.

When she looked at Corbin his lips were twitching and he said in a strangled voice, 'Prince Charming, I presume?'

In crumpled silver shirt and silver fishnet tights with a hole in the knee, she did look like the Principal Boy in a sleazy panto, and she thanked heaven for his sense of the ridiculous; at least he was smiling. She said, 'I came in through the window.'

'Without the butter?'

'It can be done.' She came out of the bathroom, her eyes darting round the living-room, and started to smile. 'Would you excuse me while I fetch my skirt?' As she reached the door, she added, 'You wouldn't lock me out?'

'What's the use when you're coming through the window?'

Anne-Marie was not in the living-room and she was not out here either, and as Livvy ran round to the back of the house she sent a grateful prayer to her stars or her guardian angel, whoever or whatever was on her side right now and had brought Corbin up here alone.

She carried her coat and her skirt back, and stepped into her skirt as soon as she got into the house, tucking in her shirt and running her fingers through her hair. 'That's better,' she said. 'Well, tidier.'

She didn't care if he was laughing at her. She asked, 'Where's Anne-Marie? She told me you were spending Christmas together, so where is she?'

He said, 'With some friends of mine.'

'Waiting for you?'

'I came back to collect a gift I'd forgotten.'

'It must have been important.'

'Fairly.'

The table in the kitchenette was laid for two, so they were coming back here, but now Corbin was alone. This could be her last chance and she had to be clever and careful, and she couldn't face him or she would be neither. She moved around, pacing the room slowly, looking everywhere except at him. 'I've brought you a present,' she said. 'I got thinking. All those things you've given me over the years and I've never given you anything, so I've brought you a present. Me.'

She looked at him then and away again at once, because he said nothing. She went on with her slow walking, and fast talking. 'You said I was too good at acting, but I wasn't acting, I was falling in love with you, and even if you don't believe that, what do you think I'm doing now? I'm not acting now—why should I be acting? I love you, and you ought to be loving me, because Anne-Marie can give you nothing compared to what we could have had together. And because some man who was your best friend was fooled by a woman, does it mean——?'

'My father,' he said. That silenced her. 'He was my father and she was my mother.' He was turning on another bar of the gas fire, his back was towards her, and she went to him. He said, 'I'd known for a long time that she was cheating, I think he did too, but when she left he had a coronary and died.'

Livvy said huskily, 'I'm so sorry.'

'So was she—she never did mean to hurt anyone, she simply got a better offer. I'm fond of her, we keep in touch, but he was my best friend as well as my father, and it changed my way of life.'

His eyes met hers and she couldn't bear to see the loneliness in them. She said gently, 'Don't let it spoil our lives. Please don't go yet. Let's stay here, just for an hour or so.' She laid her hand against his cheek in a touch that was asking for nothing, only the chance to comfort, and her lips curved. 'I could get lucky, it could start to snow.'

If it did it would not be heavy enough to hold them here, but Corbin smiled back at her and they were friends, and that was more than she could have hoped for an hour ago.

He said, 'A glass of wine?'

'Please.' She sat on the sofa, watching him as he put glasses and a bottle on a tray. 'Food?' he asked. 'Or have you been eating all day?'

'Serving mostly.' She had picked a little, she hadn't been hungry. 'Yes, please,' she said. 'Fruit, cheese, anything that's easy. My appetite is suddenly much healthier than it's been lately.'

He grinned at her and they were fooling again, and now there was no anger. They sat on the sofa, sipping their wine in the kind of companionable silence they had known before Daisy had showed Corbin the sketch.

Perhaps Livvy was being too hopeful, but it was so good like this that Anne-Marie seemed no more of a threat than Andrew. They were like shadows outside while Livvy was in here with Corbin, and the nearness of him was a warmth reaching deep inside her, as though she was drawing in life from being close to him.

She sipped her wine and ate an apple and said, 'You know what I did with all the birthday presents you gave me?'

'A bonfire or a jumble sale?'

'No. I put them all in an old tin trunk in the attic. I thought I was hiding them for ever, but I was only putting them away where they were safe. I shall go up there and fetch them all down again. Was the package you left for Aunt Maysie a Laurence Charles?'

'Yes.'

'A new one?' He nodded. 'She'll like that. And Henry's is rum? I always give him book tokens because he can't get enough books, but he could well prefer rum.'

'I had to talk to his friends to find out where he gets the stuff. I'm not surprised it isn't on general sale.'

She laughed. 'It should carry a health warning!'

She reached for a biscuit out of a tin of shortbread and Corbin said, 'There should have been a jardinière from Luke, but the man who's looking out for me is still trying the match the old one. If we can't get a match, it will have to be a near thing.'

'Thank you, Luke.' The dog, lying full length behind the sofa, thumped his tail, acknowledging his name. 'You're very thoughtful. Anne-Marie chose Sonia's and mine, didn't she?'

'She offered, yes. I thought that was thoughtful of her.'

Livvy's eyebrows rose and a quirk of his lips answered her. Anne-Marie's motives had not been all heart. 'Thermal vests.'

'Were they?'

'Don't you know the difference?'

'I'm not too well informed on vests.'

'Well, there are vests and vests.' She reached over the back of the sofa to offer Luke what was left of the biscuit, and after a few sniffs he accepted and bolted it. 'I could have shown you the difference if I'd been wearing one.'

She began to unbutton her shirt. She had already offered herself in words, but now her fingers were shaking so that she fumbled with the buttons, and her heart was thumping so hard that it hurt.

Her face burned hot as she slipped the shirt from her shoulders and unfastened the pretty lacy bra. Her skin was smooth and soft and her breasts were firm, and Corbin had seen her naked more than once. But never for him. He said huskily, 'You must have the most beautiful body in the world,' which wasn't so, but he could make it come true. With him she could be the most beautiful woman.

Shyness came over her so that she half turned away, and he touched her back. 'What's that?'

It smarted, and she remembered. 'I got stuck in your window.' She felt the light trail of his lips down her spine, and let her head fall forward and closed her eyes.

He said, 'I don't know where they get this idea that you don't need looking after. The last time you came up here you blacked out, this time you draw blood. You're going through your nine lives at a cracking pace!'

She would not be surprised if he healed her, so that when she looked in a mirror there wouldn't be a blemish on her. She murmured, 'Do you care?'

He turned her to face him and said, 'I can't risk you losing any more. If you're on the ninth, I've got to make it good and lasting.'

'I'd like that,' she said, and she slipped down in his arms so that they lay together by the fire. There was a rug on the floor, and if it was a hard bed she didn't notice. She looked up into his face and saw the light and the shadows as his hands moved over her, gently and surely. She traced his mouth with her fingertips and they made a feast of each other, touching and tasting, moving together tenderly, as though they would cherish each other all their lives.

And then there was a moment when they lay still, looking into each other's eyes, and desire rose in her with frightening and mounting intensity so that the gentle touch was not enough. She needed him closer, in her, part of her. Through clenched teeth she moaned, 'Love me,' and when he did every nerve in her leapt into avid life.

No real skill or experience, just letting him take her into the ecstasy and the agony. Sometimes not knowing which, but all of it was wonderful, and every time she thought she could go no further she was soaring again to another rapturous height until she had to be higher than the stars. Until the universe exploded and she felt like the last star of all, floating down in a million shining pieces.

She lay exhausted, too spent at first to open her eyes, but happier than she had believed possible. Then very slowly she moved her shoulders and stretched her arms above her head, delighting in the miracle of her woman's body. It was beautiful, and the man, who was so right in every way, was the most glorious man on earth.

Her eyelids were heavy. She could feel the weight of her lashes when she opened her eyes to look up at him, where he lay beside her, head propped up on an elbow, looking down. He said, 'Thank you,' and smiled. 'For my Christmas present.'

Livvy smiled back. 'You were *very* welcome.'

Her discarded clothes were close to hand. She pulled skimpy pants up over long legs and, reaching for her bra, was seized by an impish impulse. Lashes fluttering, shoulders, arms, and hips swaying, she did a burlesque striptease in reverse, putting on instead of taking off, ending barelegged but dressed and giving a final swirl in her floating skirt before she sank down on the sofa and asked, 'How's that?'

'Eat your heart out, Salome,' Corbin smiled. 'But she hadn't thought of putting on the seven veils instead of taking them off. Much sexier.'

'Oh, I like to be different.' She felt quite idiotic with happiness. 'I have surprises in store for you,' although it was herself she was surprising.

'I always knew you were talented,' he said. 'But I didn't know you had star quality as a dancer. You're not expecting me to prance around getting dressed, are you?' She pealed with laughter, as he dressed quickly.

She thought, you surprise me, I never knew love-making was so incredible because I was never in love before, and you want me, and that will always be a most amazing thing.

As he sat down beside her, she said, 'We're friends now?'

'We always were. You could have counted on me and I would have come.'

But she might not have known that, and she said, 'I'm glad I came here.' She curled up against him, his arm around her, her head in the hollow of his shoulder-blade, and told him, 'I've been in a daze. Until tonight when I was driving off with Andrew and I suddenly woke up and thought, this isn't right. Do you understand?'

'I should—it was the same with me. I was only half alive without you. The script's going well, Hedley's enthusiastic about everything and we did some good work, but I got no joy out of it.'

Surely she couldn't be jealous now, but she had to ask, 'No joy from Anne-Marie?'

'Not a lot.' When she raised her head, he met her gaze with a wry grin, then he said, 'Will you sit for the painting of the Dark Lady? We want one for the filming.'

'Why me?'

'Because Maybelle looked like you. When I knew she and Laurence were lovers that summer, I knew there couldn't have been another woman.'

Livvy let that sink in with all it implied. She said, 'You are clever.'

'I'm lucky.'

'Me, too.' She would have been scared to be so lucky if it hadn't been fate, because it was so right. 'Luckier than Maybelle. Laurence wasn't so lucky either.'

Corbin said, 'Nor clever. It shouldn't have ended like that.'

'What should he have done?' Maybelle had made her choice and her passage was booked. 'What would you have done?'

She turned now to look at him as she listened, because what could Laurence have done? And Corbin told her, 'I wouldn't have raved like he did, nor got drunk. But I'd have been on that boat next day and I'd have been with her all the way to America, and I'd have docked with her when Edward met her.'

He would not have given up. Livvy said, 'That would have changed the story. She might have married Laurence.'

'She might have done. Would you marry me?'

'Yes, please.'

The thought of being married to Corbin filled her with joy, and he said fervently, 'Thank heaven for that!' as if he had feared she might hesitate. 'When?'

'As soon as you like.'

'That's as soon as possible.'

Livvy said, 'Yes, please,' again. Wedding rings would be the outward sign that they were committed to each other body and soul, although they both knew that already. Tomorrow they would have to share their secret, tell everybody. Andrew would be upset for a while and everyone at Sweet Orchard would be thrilled. All her friends would be staggered, and she would be meeting friends of Corbin's for the first time.

But this night was precious because here they were truly alone. 'Shall we stay here tonight?'

'Let's do that.'

They had hours and hours for loving and talking. Corbin was looking at her as if everything about her was wonderful, but she felt grimy and dishevelled, and she asked, 'Can I freshen up?'

'Surely,' he said. 'I'll show you around.'

She had never been farther than the top of the stairs. There was a room up there that he must have shared with Anne-Marie, and she did not want to look in there, although it shouldn't matter much now.

In the bathroom she saw that, what with one thing and another, the make-up she had applied this morning had been thoroughly mussed, and she washed hands and face, coming up from the towel shining clean. The glow of happiness brightened her eyes and her skin so that she hardly needed make-up, which was just as well, as she hadn't any.

Then she turned on the taps to fill the bath with enough water to paddle in. She was sitting on the side of the bath, swishing her feet, smiling to herself because Corbin was waiting for her, when she remembered that his friends were waiting for him.

She stretched out a hand to open the door slightly and call, 'Corbin?'

'Yes?'

'When you don't go back, will they come looking for you?'

She would rather they did not, of course, but she couldn't see Anne-Marie staying meekly where he left her till morning. He said, 'Nobody will come looking for me. No one's expecting me anywhere.'

Livvy swung her legs out of the bath and padded wet-footed into the living-room. In the kitchenette Luke looked up briefly from his food bowl and Corbin put a white candle on a red enamel candlestick in the middle of the table. Livvy asked, 'Isn't Anne-Marie with your friends?'

'Probably with people I know.' He lit the candle. They had eaten by candlelight on their first date, she would always love candlelight. 'But not on the Island.'

'Do go on.'

He seemed to be satisfied with the table. He sat down at it, lounging in that relaxed way she knew so well. He said, 'She took the helicopter. I didn't know she was considering a change of plan until we'd parked and she said, "Leave my luggage". Val and Hedley made themselves scarce and Anne-Marie said, "Something or someone on this island has changed you," and I couldn't argue with that when I'd just spent two celibate nights with her.'

Livvy was delighted to hear it. She held down a whoop of triumph and said shakily, 'That couldn't have been easy.'

'It was awkward. Fortunately, I do have this reputation of being a cold fish.'

'Not true.' She had to laugh at that.

'It can be when you're not around. Anyhow, she gave me an ultimatum. She'd stay if I'd take real notice of her, instead of carrying on as if I had something else on my mind.'

You don't listen to me, you don't see me, Andrew had said. They were both outsiders...

Corbin said, 'Otherwise she was off and it was over,' and Livvy went to the table to sit facing him.

'And?'

He said, 'There never had been anything more than affection, occasional sex, interests and friends we shared.'

'Some might call that love.' Marriages could last a lifetime on less, but for those who were truly blessed there was so much more.

Corbin said quietly, 'Once I might have called it love, but I could never have called it commitment. Now I know them both and I want them both because they will make life worth living.'

Livvy's eyes misted. 'What did you say to her?'

'I said goodbye, and she said, "I suppose it's Livvy. You know my number".'

That was no ultimatum. Anne-Marie hoped this was only a casual affair, and Livvy was secure and happy enough to feel sorry for her. Corbin said, 'She went with Val and Hedley and I came back here, set two places at table and waited until your party was almost over. Then I went to fetch you.'

She echoed, 'Fetch me?'

'That's right. I thought you might expect an apology, perhaps an explanation, but I thought you'd come. Only you'd gone with Andrew to somebody else's party. When I got there Andrew was drowning his sorrows. He didn't seem to be enjoying himself, and you, I was told, had had a headache and couldn't come. It took about two minutes to get out of him that you'd made him stop the car and were last seen climbing the hill.'

'Hey,' said Livvy, 'hold it!' She jumped up. 'You were coming for me, but you let me believe you were like this with Anne-Marie.' She waved two fingers tight-crossed together at him. 'So I did all that pleading, all that begging—I was nearly on my knees!'

'Rubbish!'

'Well, as near as.' He had certainly misled her. 'You said she was waiting for you.' But of course she was. Like Andrew. 'And that you'd come back for a present you'd forgotten. Now that *was* a lie.'

'Sorry,' he said, 'but I couldn't resist listening to you saying your piece. And I was the one who proposed. It's the first time I've ever done that, and I was scared you were going to come up with some reason why it wasn't a good idea.'

Livvy flounced away from the table. 'I would have done if I'd known, I'd have made you sweat a bit. As it was, I couldn't say yes fast enough. If you hadn't asked me, I could have been asking you before the night was through.'

Corbin got up too, coming round the table towards her. 'I'm sorry I missed that. Would you have said you weren't worthy of me?'

'I would not!' She produced a glare, shaking her fall of hair over her face, and he stopped dead.

'The Siamese squint! Is it stress or love?' He was smiling, laughing, and so of course was she.

'This much stress,' she said, finger and thumb a fraction apart. 'And this much love.'

She flung her arms wide for him and, as he reached her and scooped her into his arms, she looked up towards the top of the stairs.

'Blow out the candle,' she said.

HARLEQUIN
Romance®

Coming Next Month

Available in March wherever paperback books are sold, or through Harlequin Reader Service:

In the U.S.
901 Fuhrmann Blvd.
P.O. Box 1397
Buffalo, N.Y. 14240-1397

In Canada
P.O. Box 603
Fort Erie, Ontario
L2A 5X3

You'll flip . . . your pages won't!
Read paperbacks *hands-free* with

Book Mate · I

The perfect "mate" for all your romance paperbacks

**Traveling • Vacationing • At Work • In Bed • Studying
• Cooking • Eating**

Perfect size for all standard paperbacks, this wonderful invention makes reading a pure pleasure! Ingenious design holds paperback books OPEN and FLAT so even wind can't ruffle pages — leaves your hands free to do other things. Reinforced, wipe-clean vinyl-covered holder flexes to let you turn pages without undoing the strap . . . supports paperbacks so well, they have the strength of hardcovers!

Pages turn WITHOUT opening the strap.

SEE-THROUGH STRAP

Reinforced back stays flat.

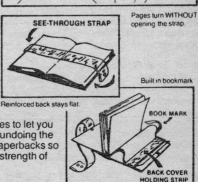

Built in bookmark

BOOK MARK

BACK COVER HOLDING STRIP

10˝ x 7¼˝, opened.
Snaps closed for easy carrying, too

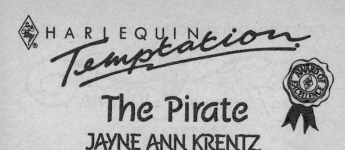

The Pirate
JAYNE ANN KRENTZ

At the heart of every powerful romance story lies a
legend. There are many romantic legends and
countless modern variations on them, but they all
have one thing in common: They are tales of brave,
resourceful women who must gentle and tame the
powerful, passionate men who are their true mates.

The enormous appeal of Jayne Ann Krentz lies in
her ability to create modern-day versions of these
classic romantic myths, and her LADIES AND
LEGENDS trilogy showcases this talent. Believing
that a storyteller who can bring legends to life
deserves special attention, Harlequin has chosen
the first book of the trilogy—THE PIRATE—to
receive our Award of Excellence. Look for it now.

AE-PIR-1A

February brings you . . .

valentine's night

Sorrel didn't particularly want to meet her long-lost cousin Val from Australia. However, since the girl had come all this way just to make contact, it seemed a little churlish not to welcome her.

As there was no room at home, it was agreed that Sorrel and Val would share the Welsh farmhouse that was being renovated for Sorrel's brother and his wife. Conditions were a bit primitive, but that didn't matter.

At least, not until Sorrel found herself snowed in with the long-lost cousin, who turned out to be a handsome, six-foot male!

Also, look for the next Harlequin Presents Award of Excellence title in April:

Elusive as the Unicorn
by Carole Mortimer

HP1243-1